# Von Mozar

## SEXFIEND

**WATERBUCK PUBLISHING LIMITED**

LONDON, UK

First published in Great Britain in 2006
by WATERBUCK PUBLISHING

ISBN 0 9548630 2 X

Printed and bound in Great Britain by
BookMarque

Typesetting: Waterbuck Publishing

Photography: Calina Zadravetz
Cover photo: Posed by models
All rights reserved

WATERBUCK PUBLISHING LIMITED
Waterbuck House, Office 125,
14 Tottenham Court Road
London W1T 1JY

WWW.WATERBUCK.CO.UK

**CAUTION:** This piece of literature is written in UK street slang.

If you are unfamiliar with any words or phrases, please refer to the glossary at the back.

# SEXFIEND

To Pauline

One love

Von Dabbar

27/6/07

*Dedicated to the girl I met in 98 but first saw in the park in 97*

*And to everyone who bought and enjoyed Ignorance Kills...*

*Peace.*

*Von Mozar aka Nicke Nicks*

# PROLOGUE

# RUNDOWN HOUSING ESTATE

# Chapter I

**THE LARGE DOUBLE ROOM** is quiet. Seven sleeping bodies fill it.

Eschewal, twelve years old, lays on a bed with his auntie, who is four years his senior, baby brother and sister. The bed opposite occupies his three older brothers.

The nudging signal comes to him. He knows what it means, tries to ignore it, but she won't let him. Her hot breath blows down his left ear as she speaks.

"Oi, you wanna do it?" she says in a whisper.

Eschewal wants to tell her no but she persists, with her big thighs.

"Oi, Eros are you sleeping?"

Eschewal pretends he is and lets out a moan, but she continues.

"Hey, Eros do you want to do it?"

He answers dumbly: "Mmmm, what did you say?"

"Do you want to do it?" she replies.

Eschewal dumbly persists. "What... Now?!"

"Yeah, come on, man, please," she pleads.

Butterflies begin to swirl in Eschewal's stomach.

Reluctantly he climbs on top and meets with his aunty's half-naked body. She pulls down his Y fronts then guides his penis into her vagina. He places his head onto her young firm breasts and begins bouncing up and down, her hot breath blows down his ear as she moans and groans.

Eschewal buries his face in the mattress as the sex becomes more intense. The next experience is new to him but not that new that he didn't know it was coming. His butt cheeks clench as he ejaculates.

They carry on pumping for a while longer. She squeals for a moment or two, then before Eschewal can slip off she pushes him off. Eschewal rolls onto his back then rolls over onto his front.

Slowly, the same sickening feeling he always feels after sexing his aunt runs though his bones and makes him feel sinful, filthy, even evil. In this moment he wishes he could rip his insides out and not be the person whom he is; not have to live in poverty, and experience the horror he experiences.

Eschewal wants to cry but holds the tears because the worst thing about the experience is when it begins and before it ends, it makes him feel beautiful inside. And this beauty is more powerful than the sickening after-effects.

Eschewal finally close his eyes, hoping this haunting was another one of those dreams.

# EIGHT YEARS LATER

# Chapter II

**ESCHEWAL TOSSES AND TURNS** then shoots open his eyes. He has sweat running down his face and his heart is racing. He grabs his penis, which is rock hard, then realizes the haunting is one of those neurotic dreams he has from time to time.

Eschewal begins to panic as he finds himself handcuffed to a hospital bed. Earlier he had been knocked down as he tried to escape from the boy-dem.

He looks to his left and two other beds come into view. The one in the middle is empty but its sheets are ruffled. The one at the end is neatly made up. He looks towards the ceiling and closes his eyes.

Eschewal has had enough of the street life, had enough of being chased by the boy-dem. He has had enough of being locked up in cells and most of all he has had enough of feeling pain. Tears come to his eyes as nothing comes to his mind on how to escape the grime that he's been trapped in, since the days he started having sex with his aunty.

Eschewal whispers to himself: *"Why?"* Before he can repeat, *why me?* a flood of tears from the entire repressed pain, anger and ignorance roll down his face. As Eschewal bawls, he loses himself and slips into his own private world and all sounds from the past and the present are blocked out. While there Eschewal wishes someone could show him how to find happiness. All he really wants is to lead a good life that involves marriage, kids and a job.

Gently in the background, the sound of music and a powerful light voice shakes Eschewal out of his semi-consciousness.

"Do you want me to call someone, son?" repeats the voice.

Eschewal opens his eyes but doesn't answer. The voice continues to question: "What are all those tears for?"

Eschewal remains quiet. The voice continues: "I bet I can guess why you're crying. You wish you could have the nice things in life without experiencing any pain."

That sentence gets Eschewal's full attention. He wipes his tears and focuses on the old man's wrinkled face and strong youthful eyes, which reflect genuine honesty.

The old man stares at Eschewal before continuing. "What if I told you that the words in this book," the old man removes a medium size black book from under his pillow, "hold the key to make you happy, rich and powerful enough to never again feel pain. Would you believe me?"

Eschewal speaks for the first time: "I don't know, does it?"

"Yes it does, and much more, just as long as you read it and use the knowledge. But remember whatever you learn you don't need to believe, you need to accept."

Eschewal laughs lightly, holds his waist and screws his face from the pain as he sits up. "Listen, I don't read books!" he exclaims.

The old man nods his head. "I know you don't read. Most people where you come from don't either. That's why most experience a life of pain and hardship."

The old man rises slightly from the bed and extends the book towards Eschewal. "Take it, read the book."

Eschewal leaves the old man hanging, he is intrigued so he questions: "But why give me the book?"

The old man smiles and simply says: "I have finished with it, I no longer need it."

Eschewal extends his hand but is restricted by the handcuffs. The old man stretches closer and says: "Remember, the use of knowledge is power!" then drops the book into Eschewal's hand.

Suddenly a strange feeling comes over Eschewal, the old man continues talking but Eschewal doesn't hear, his thoughts are captivated by the book's title.

**HOW TO CREATE YOUR DESTINY AND FOR-EVER LIVE LIFE WITH HAPPINESS & RICHES**

Eschewal looks up towards the old man for an explanation of the title, but the old man has already left the room. This leaves Eschewal without a choice. He opens the book to the first page and begins reading.

# Chapter III

**ESCHEWAL READS THE FIRST** line of the book.

*You're the creator of your own destiny.*

Surprise dons Eschewal's face. He licks his lips and continues reading.

*For over 2000 years destructive-governments have blocked the immense power, which dwells within every human mind from unleashing.*

Eschewal removes his eyes from the page and blinks towards the ceiling. He wonders what could be this immense power that dwells within. His heart is pounding. He takes a deep breath and continues reading.

*That immense power is the full use of one's consciousness. What is consciousness? Consciousness is the ability to debate with oneself, make decisions and ultimately create new values. One can only create new values once one has learned how to unleash one's full consciousness.*

Eschewal places the book on his chest and closes his eyes. He knows the next thing the book will tell him is how to unleash his consciousness, so hurriedly he continues.

*To unleash one's full consciousness, one must disconnect from the destructive matrix of corrupt forces by rejecting anything that destroys the human organism, whether mental or physical. The following are the most common.*

Eschewal slowly begins to read aloud the list he must disconnect from: *Sugar, Alcohol, Caffeine, Tobacco, Narcotics, Promiscuity, Objective-Crime, Gambling, Destructive-Governments, Mysticism and Cults.*

The book continues: *Once disconnected from those destructive forces, you will unleash the full power of your consciousness. This will give you the ability to become a creator of values. Then, automatically, happiness & riches will flow to you.*

A feeling of excitement seeps through Eschewal as he is promised happiness & riches. Eschewal smiles because all his life he dreamt of happiness and enough money to get out of the ghetto. Therefore, the decision to believe what the book promises is an easy one.

Eschewal lays the book on his chest and plans to disconnect from the list of destructive forces, one by one.

# PART ONE

# FIVE YEARS LATER

# Chapter One

**ESCHEWAL SITS AT HIS** desk in a shirt and tie staring at his computer screen. It's taken a while but Eschewal has disconnected from all the destructive forces. The last destructive force, which Eschewal disconnected from, was promiscuous sex. This was the hardest one because Eschewal had always been in conflict with the man side of him versus the dog. The dog in him had made him do terrible things in the past and always made him feel sick and twisted afterwards. So when he had learnt what promiscuity meant, he was glad he had to fight the dog and get rid of it to become a creator of values and receive the happiness & riches the black book promised. Two years after killing the dog in him Eschewal is now waiting to become a creator of values but unfortunately Eschewal had not understood clearly the second requirement in achieving this. He had thought by just reading the book and disconnecting from all the destructive forces, he would automatically become a creator of values and receive happiness & riches. But this has not happened and Eschewal is wondering why.

He thinks back to that night he laid in the hospital bed. He did not sleep until he completed the whole book. From that very first page the book drew him into a world outside of himself. As he read more of the book he was hit by words he had never seen before. They were strange words, but within sentences amongst other common words he had just about understood the message and the power of the book. Once he reached the end of the book the book warned him: *Be careful whom you expose this knowledge to because many will become angry (even though they implicitly know reality) and quickly defend the destructive matrix of corrupt forces with a hundred different rationalisations. These people do not want to be disconnected because the corrupt forces provide short-term happiness (which leads to long-term problems). Remember, most people are willing to trade their health and life in exchange for destructive stimulation.*

Eschewal smiles and begins to shut down his computer. He has to admit that since the moment he decided to disconnect from the destructive forces, his life has been much better. He shakes his head at still not understanding why he has not yet become a creator of values.

Eschewal rises from his desk unaware that the answer to his question will soon reveal itself, but not before taking him though the dark depths of his soul.

# Chapter Two

**AT FIVE TO SIX,** Eschewal has already left the building. As he steps outside the cool fresh air hits him and seems to shake off the oppressive stress of the office. He begins to smile because he has a definite link for later on. Her name is Keneisha. Eschewal had met her four months ago. He had taken her out on two expensive dates, without getting as much as a kiss. This didn't matter now because all week Keneisha had been promising Eschewal he would get lucky at the weekend. This promise was what got him through his gruelling working week. A wider smile dons Eschewal's face as he bops past a row of shop fronts. His phone begins to ring. It's Keneisha. Butterflies swirl around his stomach, he hopes she's calling to tell him to pick her up earlier.

Eschewal answers the phone with his controlled sexy voice: "Yeah what's up, Keneisha?"

Keneisha's voice drops a tone, she says: "Oh babes, I'm so sorry, I can't make it again."

For a second Eschewal loses his voice, hot heat raises inside of him, those words feel like the impact of a car crash, resulting in his whole world collapsing. A lump appears in his throat, but Eschewal controls his voice and replies: "Yeah, why doh?"

"Oh at the last minute, I've been asked to babysit my goddaughter. You understand, don't you?"

Eschewal replies yes, which is a lie because he doesn't understand. *'How could she do me like this?'* thinks Eschewal.

Keneisha ends the call with the promise that she will link Eschewal tomorrow; another lie. She has a better link for later on and tomorrow, so Keneisha's 'goddaughter' is really Godfrey, a big time shotter who has a mansion in the countryside.

For a moment Eschewal feels disorientated. He slips the phone into his pocket. Then loudly, his pet name (which everyone knows him by except loved ones and the boy-dem) is hollered from across the street.

"Oi, Eros, you listening?"

*"Oh shit, it's Tek,"* says Eschewal to himself.

Back in the day, Tek was always thinking up new ways on how to make illegal money but his ideas always seemed to get Eschewal arrested whenever he decided to go on a move with Tek.

Tek calls again.

*"Arh, what the hell does he want, man? I bet he wants to ask if I'm down with one of his bait moves."* says Eschewal to himself. Eschewal screws his face and thinks. *'But I'm sure he knows I don't make money off the road no more.'* Eschewal sucks on his teeth and thinks. *'Its taken me five years to break away from the road, so why does this waste-man wanna drag me back down?'*

Eschewal raises one finger in the air and shouts back at Tek: "Just cool, man, I'm in rush. What are you still on the same number?"

Tek nods his head.

"Alright, man I'll ding you little more from now." Tek raises his right hand in the air. Eschewal nods his head and raises his fist then turns down the first road on his right with no intentions of ever phoning Tek.

# Chapter Three

ESCHEWAL'S MIND IS SPINNING. He feels like calling Keneisha back and begging her to link him, when his pet name is hollered once again. This time from the top of a bedroom window. He looks up and spots another thug that he grew up with. Deuce is his name, a natural fighter with overgrown muscles, medium in height with a face that is a bit too pretty for a man.

Eschewal's heart begins to pound. He cannot remember the reason why he and Deuce stopped moving, it might have been over beef. Eschewal licks his lips and controls his voice trying not to show his fear.

"Yeah, what's going on, bro?"

"Boy nuffing, cuz. Oi, wait there I'm gonna come down and rap to you."

At that moment Eschewal's legs begin to shake. His arms go dead. His mind tells his legs to run, his legs don't respond. His male pride kicks in. He tells himself: *"Come on, bruv don't be a punk."* Eschewal shakes his head and wonders: *'What happened to that killer instinct? Has that black book turned me into a pussy?'*

Eschewal thinks hard on those thoughts then realises that the black book has not only made him value his own life; it has made him value lives of others also. Eschewal's thoughts break as the front door opens. Deuce comes charging out. Eschewal holds his breath waiting to block the impact from a punch. Deuce's arms extend towards Eschewal, and embrace him with a handshake and a hug. "What's up, blud? I ain't seen you for long, cuz. What's going on, man? What's popping? What's good?"

Eschewal pulls back and looks square into Deuce's eyes wanting to see if he is for real. Eschewal can't tell, so he plays along.

"Just chilling, bruv, man's working now, you get me?"

Deuce releases his grip on Eschewal and replies: "Yeah. Man's working too, fam. You feel me? I left the grime, road's too sticky it's a long-ting."

Eschewal begins to smile as he relaxes. "Course, course, cuz the streets are long, blud, you dun know. So where you working now anyway?"

Deuce sucks on his teeth then answers: "I sell phones, blud, trust me it's all right, blud. You know how much chicks man's slapped from the time I've been selling phones."

"Yeah, true stories?" says Eschewal, as he grows a wide smile on his face, remembering that Deuce had always been a girl's man.

"Yeah, bruv, one's coming down right now, bruv. I sold her a heavy phone and gave her a good deal, you feel me, player? Course." Deuce rubs his chin, he has an idea. He points at Eschewal. "Oi, you know what, though, bruv? This ting is a little freak, cuz. Man can battery it, standard."

Eschewal's eyes widen, as he remembers taking part in a few batteries back in the day. He had always hated doing them because he never did like having unemotional sex. It always made him feel dirty afterwards and not only that, there was always a chance that the girl would call rape.

Eschewal looks Deuce in his eyes and wants to say no, but the whole week of anticipating some good sex has woken the dog. It starts barking, raging and foaming at the mouth. Butterflies consume him, he becomes light headed.

"Yeah, true stories, yeah, she's up for battery?" asks Eschewal smoothly.

"Course, bruv, I'm not gonna lie to you." Deuce opens his door and invites Eschewal in.

Eschewal steps into the house saying: "Yeah, man, I'm down," with words from the black book stinging through his mind.

*Having promiscuous sex lowers ones self-esteem through the effect of short-term happiness, which leads to long-term problems.*

# Chapter Four

**AS THE DOOR CLOSES** behind Eschewal, Deuce's phone begins to ring. "Yeah, hello," he says then pokes Eschewal's shoulder to get his attention. Eschewal looks towards him. Deuce pulls the phone away from his mouth and whispers to Eschewal: "It's her, blud."

Deuce puts the phone back to his ear. "Yeah, yeah, babes," he continues, "take the first right then the second left and you'll be on my road. Come to 108... yeah, alright."

Deuce ends the call then shouts: "Rudeboy, she's round the corner, blud!"

He pushes open a door and tells Eschewal to follow. Eschewal is led into a large room with minimal furniture. Only a long chair and a table are inside the badly decorated walls.

"Yeah, blud. You listening? This is how we're gonna run it. When she comes, yeah, you wait in here and don't make her see you. I'll bring her straight to my room and go thru, then tell her I'm gonna take a piss. That's when you go in and kill it."

Eschewal thinks for a second, and decides that plan doesn't sound good. "Nah, bro that sound like no battery, that's a long-ting."

Deuce shuts his eyes then opens them and shrugs his shoulders. "How? It's not long, what's wrong with you, man? Listen this chick is dumb and the room is gonna be dark, so when you go in just act like you're me, init."

Eschewal pauses in thought, but before he can run through the possible consequences of his actions Deuce's phone rings. He answers.

The girl is outside. He clicks off his phone then says: "So what are you saying?" Before Eschewal can answer he adds: "You're down, man, just cool," then leaves the room.

Eschewal runs to the window-curtain and peeps though. Subconsciously he licks his lips as he sees the girl walking towards the door. Eschewal's penis grows hard, the dog begins howling after this firm young body. Images of him sexing her floods his mind. At that moment Eschewal knows the animal in him has won and all the wrong that he is about to do gets pushed aside.

# Chapter Five

**BEFORE ESCHEWAL KNOWS IT,** he is standing in the dark room looking over at the girl. She calls to him: "Oi, babes, you took long in the bathroom, man."

Eschewal's heart skips a beat. He pushes his chest out before he answers, and with the best impersonation of Deuce, he says: "Just cool, man. What you ready for the second round?"

The girl wriggles her body on the bed and says: "What do you think?"

Eschewal smiles and steps forward. "Alright then, turn around."

The girl rises to her knees and turns her backside towards Eschewal. His heart now begins to pound, butterflies swirl, he can't believe it's working. Eschewal calms himself then begins to rub his hand over her backside.

"Oh flip, you're so sexy." The girl stops her winding and looks over her shoulder as if the sentence Eschewal said didn't sound like something Deuce would have said. Before she can take any other action Eschewal thinks quickly and sticks his fingers into her vagina, she moans and grips the sheets.

Adrenalin runs through Eschewal, he thinks: *'I need to put it in quick enough so she won't pull away and get a better look at my face.'* With his free hand, Eschewal unzips his flies. His penis jumps out. He dips into his back pocket slips out a condom and bites it open, then rolls it on.

He then positions his penis towards the girl's unexpecting vagina and in one swift movement he removes his fingers then penetrates. The girl shoots forward, he grips her waist and pulls her back. Then faster and faster he slides in and out. The girl moans and begins to slowly crawl forward. By now, Eschewal is in his own world trying to quickly buss-a-nut. Eschewal opens his eyes and realises the girl has reached the curtain and is pulling it open to let in the evening sun, so she can see his face. Eschewal panics and falls forward onto the girl. He shakes a little as if he's ejaculating. The girl lets go of the curtain. Eschewal removes his penis, then says: "Yeah, babes I've come."

The girl quickly springs around towards Eschewal but all she sees is the back of his shadow leaving the room.

# Chapter Six

**OUTSIDE THE ROOM, DEUCE** had been playing with himself as he listened to Eschewal sexing. Deuce ejaculated in his left palm and is now in the bathroom washing his hand off.

Eschewal stands in the hallway not knowing where to go, his hands are sweating. With his mind racing he hopes the girl doesn't bust out of the bedroom.

The bathroom door opens and Deuce peeps out. "Oi Eros, come," he says.

Eschewal rubs his hands on his trousers and walks in the bathroom.

Deuce closes the door. "Yes, blud, I heard you killing, cuz."

Eschewal jumps into the player role: "Course, course, blud, I mashed dat down," he states with a fake laugh and a smile. Really he feels disgusted and wishes he could reverse time.

Deuce lets out a silly sounding high-pitched laugh then hits his fist on Eschewal's. Eschewal puts on his serious face, then says: "Oi, you know what doh, I think she knew it wasn't you, rudeboy. I swear down, blud she try buss the curtain on man, so I had to all sink it deeper until she let go of it, blud."

Before Deuce can respond, the girl hollers for him. Deuce opens the bathroom door and shouts back: "I'm just in the bathroom. Wait there I'm coming."

Deuce closes the door and turns to Eschewal. A cunning thought comes to him. He needs a lift-boy to drive him to meet different links because his wifey almost caught him with one of his girls in his car.

"Listen, bruv, don't watch dat, she's some dumb bitch. She don't know nothing, so just cool, man, everyting is jiggy." Deuce leads Eschewal out of the bathroom.

Eschewal follows up behind and says: "Alright, gee."

Deuce turns to Eschewal and whispers: "Oi, rudeboy, let me get your number." Deuce pulls out his phone and punches in Eschewal's number. Deuce points towards the front door. "Yeah just creep out, yeah. I'll give you a one ding and you'll get my number." Eschewal nods his head, Deuce again whispers: "Alright, blud we link, yeah?" He then hits his fist onto Eschewal's once more then steps into his bedroom.

Deuce switches on the bedroom light and quickly runs game. "Whats up, babes? How you screaming out my name like that? I'm a man not a machine, you know."

The girl squints her eyes, and then smirks. "Um, is there anyone else in the house, Mark, uh?" she questions with suspicion in her voice.

Mark is the alias that Deuce gave the girl. He screws

his face. "How you mean if there's someone else in the house?" He sucks on his teeth. "Nah it's just me and you, like who else is meant to be here?"

The girl shakes her head then retorts: "Um, no one," but within her mind she's sure that was a different penis inside her. Nothing could tell her different but she will keep it to herself for one reason: the shame of being played for a fool.

Deuce rubs his chest and turns on the TV with a cunning smile on his face. It disappears as he turns around and jumps on the bed. As he does, Eschewal turns from listening at the bedroom door. He had to be sure that the girl wasn't aware and with tremendous guilt and feeling dirty, Eschewal walks down the stairs, creeps out the front door and hits the streets.

# Chapter Seven

**"HEY? LARGE OR SMALL?"**

"Small please," replies Eschewal to the big-boned woman, behind the food counter. He gives her the payment and without a smile she hands over his change. Eschewal slips it in his pocket and takes a seat on one of the soft stools that the restaurant provides for take-away customers.

As he sits, his thoughts travel back to when he was stealing sex. Eschewal shakes his head. He cannot believe that his need to buss-a-nut drove him to the thin line between sex and rape. His heart sinks and he thinks maybe what he did was rape; his whole body turns hot. He closes his eyes and then runs through in his mind what represents a rape. He quickly reassures himself: *"I didn't force the girl; she gave it to me, but she only gave it because she thought I was Deuce. Would she have given it to me if she knew it wasn't?"* That question begins to weigh on Eschewal's mind. He looks towards his feet and shrugs off the question by telling himself: *"Yeah, man she knew it was someone else. She just played the fool so she could get sexed by two different men."*

That new idea of the situation starts to make Eschewal feel better. It makes him relax and visions of him sticking his penis in and out of the girl's vagina flood his mind. The dog crawls on his back, making his penis grow hard. The sexual pictures now flip though his mind a thousand paces a minute. He grabs his penis then remembers that he didn't ejaculate.

The dog begins to howl, the assault is too overwhelming. Eschewal bites his lip. He knows the dog is out of its cage. He shakes his head and says to himself: *"Damn, why did Keneisha have to blow me out and release this dog in me? After all that effort I put in to get rid of it."*

Eschewal closes his eyes and continues to reason with himself: *"Cha, I swear the black book is a joke. I've done everything it said and still yet I've not become a creator of values."*

Eschewal sucks his teeth and looks at his phone. He begins to flick through the contacts. *"Flip, no girls to call."* He had deleted all the girls in his phone when he decided to disconnect from promiscuous sex.

*"Arh, what am I gonna do now to release?"* Eschewal laughs to himself. *"Geez, it looks like I might have pay for a prostitute."*

Eschewal sucks his teeth. *"Nah that's long, I can't slip like that."* He looks over at the big-boned woman. He contemplates to drop a few words on to her. He tries to catch her eye as she places the lid onto his food. She doesn't look up until the food is packed into the white plastic bag.

The big-boned woman gives Eschewal the bag, without a smile.

Eschewal says: "Thank you," and takes the bag.

He turns on his heels and exits the shop with his mind spinning on how to release his sexual tension.

# Chapter Eight

**ESCHEWAL TURNS RIGHT AS** he steps out of the takeaway. He walks into the sweetie shop next door to buy a sugar-free drink. Outside the shop are two bus stops. The one furthest from the shop has a young lady standing and looking at him as he pays for his drink.

The young lady had been making her way to meet a guy but on the way he had called and said he couldn't meet her again. All week the young lady had prepared for the date; it was the one thing that got her through her stressful week at work. She had planned on giving it up on the first night. She had visions of being stretched out on a bed with her legs up in the air and her hair all messed up.

Her sights are now set firmly on Eschewal. She contemplates how to get his attention. With no time left, Eschewal steps out of the shop. The young lady's nerves give way and she takes her glare off Eschewal just quick enough for him not to have noticed that she was staring.

Eschewal notices the young lady. On first appearance she's not his usual type. She's a bit on the chunky side but she's fairly tall so she carries the chunkiness well.

Eschewal steps past her and notices that her eyes twitch towards him and in that moment he feels something in the air. Quick as a flash he sees images of her and him sexing back at his flat. The dog jumps on his back and stops him in his tracks. He dwells: *'She's just like you; all she wants is a little sexual release. Just step to her, all she can say is no.'*

Eschewal turns around, his nerves running a rampage. He heads back to the young lady, like someone who has nothing to lose.

Eschewal gets the young lady's attention. She turns around with a wide smile on her face like she's won the lotto.

"Sorry what did you say?" she questions.

Like a good actor, Eschewal hides his nervousness and repeats: "I said, what is a beautiful girl like you doing alone on a Friday night?"

The young lady smiles. "Oh I just came from visiting my grandparents. I'm just on my way home."

Eschewal nods his head. "Yeah, so what's your name anyway?"

"Camille," answers the young lady.

Eschewal has already forgotten her name. He extends his hand. "Nice to meet you, babes. My name's Eros." Eschewal doesn't let go of the young lady's hand. "So you're saying that you're just going home?"

The young lady nods her head.

"Ok, so if that's all you're doing, what would you say if I invited you around to my flat for something to eat?" Eschewal holds his breath as he waits for her reply and tries to think of something cool to say if she blows him out.

Slowly, at first, her lips begin to stretch open, revealing her white teeth. It's not yet certain if her mouth is turning up into a smile, until she says: "Yeah, alright."

Eschewal pauses for a moment and thinks: *That seemed too easy, maybe there is something wrong with this chick?'*

The dog begins barking and demands Eschewal to stop thinking. His heart skips a beat as he leads the young lady to his home.

# Chapter Nine

**ESCHEWAL HAS JUST FINISHED** eating. He is now sitting on his sofa. The TV is tuned into a video music channel. The young lady sits to his right staring at the TV.

They haven't talked much since they got in the flat and the situation seems to be growing tense. Eschewal deliberates: *'I wonder if the only way to get sex tonight is to lick it before I can stick it?'*

Eschewal looks at her glass, the drink is almost finished. He uses this as an ice breaker. "Um, would you like another drink?" he says politely.

She turns to him, smiles. "No, thank you."

Eschewal holds her stare and questions: "So what, babes, you don't have a boyfriend then?"

She bats her eyelids. "No, not at the moment. What, have you got a girl?"

Eschewal looks towards his feet. "Nah, I ain't got a girl."

The young lady's eyes glisten with hope; Eschewal doesn't notice.

Eschewal rubs his chin. "Um, babes can I ask you something?"

The young lady nods her head. "Yeah, go on."

Eschewal grins to himself. "Do you like sex?"

"Yeah, of course!" replies the young lady with a nod.

Eschewal's grin spreads wider. "So what type of sex do you like, babes?" Eschewal doesn't give her a chance to answer. "I bet you like oral?"

"Mmmm, yeah." The young lady's eyes drift off as if she's imagining her vagina being licked.

Eschewal's penis grows big and stiff, it starts to beat as his heart pumps more and more blood to it.

Eschewal leans back in the sofa and controls his eagerness, he says: "I bet you like giving it too, don't you, babes?"

The young lady licks her lips and blushes, she holds her nose and begins to laugh. Eschewal stares at her with a grin on his face.

"What?" she questions, then lets out another laugh. "Yeah, okay, I do, but it depends on who, but I rather it be given to me."

Eschewal says to himself: *"Shit, I'm sure I'm gonna have to lick it before I can stick it."* Eschewal shakes his head and decides. *"Nah it's not gonna be that type of party."* But a quick sharp bite from the dog's need to buss-a-nut tonight, makes Eschewal swallow some spit and say: "So what about if I was to offer to go down on you now, what would you say?"

The young lady doesn't say yes or nod her head, she simply smiles and slides her body further down in the chair. Eschewal grabs the waist of her skirt and pulls it and her thongs down. He slowly spreads her legs apart and sticks his face between her thighs.

# Chapter Ten

**MONDAY EVENING AND ESCHEWAL** sits at his desk bored as hell waiting for the time to hit six. His thoughts travel back to the weekend. He sees himself licking that young lady's vagina. He hates the dog in him. Eschewal clenches his teeth and feels like spitting as the smell of her vagina comes to his memory.

When the smell first hit Eschewal he wanted to scream: *"Err, it stinks!"* but couldn't bring himself to embarrass the young lady, so he held his breath, closed his eyes and licked. After the ordeal Eschewal swore he would never do oral sex again, and what made it worse was that he only did it thinking he had to, not realizing the young lady would have given him sex with or without oral.

Eschewal rubs his chin and readjusts himself in the chair. He opens and closes a few programs on his screen to make it look like he is working, then relaxes as his manager leaves the office for the day.

Eschewal sucks his teeth, knowing the dog is about to take back over his life if he doesn't do something or think of something. Eschewal shakes his head, he wishes some miracle could happen and he could become a creator of values right now.

Eschewal questions himself: *"Why? How?"* His thoughts now travel back to a section in the black book. It is a section on romantic love. It says: *One of the greatest achievements in life is finding true romantic love, then committing oneself in a monogamous relationship.*

For a moment, Eschewal's mind goes blank, and then it hits him. He thinks: *'The reason why I haven't become a creator of values is because I haven't found romantic love and began a monogamous relationship.'*

Eschewal is sure this is the reason; he did everything else the black book instructed, except this.

Eschewal tells himself: *"Yep, I'm gonna begin my search for romantic love."*

Eschewal's faith in the black book restores, the dog begins to retreat back to its cage. Eschewal feels at ease and before he can decide where to begin his search, Deuce's name flashes up on his phone.

Eschewal filps into player mode and answers: "Yeah, what's going on, bruv?"

"Nothing, man, wah gwan?"

"I'm at work init, soon finish in about ten minutes. Oi, you listening? What happen with that ting on Friday?"

"Nothing, man. She's an idiot, everything criss, man. She try question me but she never know nothing."

A smile reaches Eschewal's face. He had been agonizing all weekend over it, he now promises himself he will never do anything like that again.

"Anyway listen," begins Deuce, "what you doing on the weekend?"

"Nothing, why?"

"Boy, there's something in the park init, ber girls are gonna be there, bruv."

Another smile hits Eschewal's face. He feels this could be a perfect place to find romantic love.

"Yeah, man, I'm down. Just call me at the weekend, init."

# Chapter Eleven

**THE WEEKEND ARRIVES. THE** sun is blazing as Eschewal pushes his car into a tight parking space and switches off the engine. Deuce pops the door and says: "Come we go."

Eschewal pops his door and steps out, he slams it shut and turns on the alarm, then follows. As him and Deuce hit the park area they join a thick crowd of people, all walking towards the main stage.

The music is pumping. There are all types of food smells wafting though the air. People are jumping up and down raving to the music as they spill their drinks on themselves and other people.

Eschewal and Deuce stop on the outskirts of the massive crowd of ravers. Deuce's eyes begin to dart around at all the females. He says to himself: *"Nothing but jezzys."*

Eschewal's eyes steadily move from girl to girl, studying them like they're fine works of art on display in a gallery. Three minutes more and Eschewal would never have seen her. But in that moment when he decided to look over his shoulder, his world would never be the same again.

For a number of seconds everything around him falls silent and his eyes become transfixed on love. She stands, glowing and radiating her beauty. A sharp prick sticks him in his heart as if it is an arrow from the love cupid. Butterflies attack his stomach. His legs go weak; he seems to have lost control of his bodily functions. His heart tells him: *this is your future wife. You need to be stepping to her now.* But the fear of rejection makes Eschewal turn around to contemplate his actions. Eschewal's heart begins to beat loudly. He feels it is too good to be true, that he could find romantic love so quickly.

Eschewal begins to shake his head. He tells himself: *"I don't deserve someone as nice as her. I can't get someone like her, and she'll probably have a boyfriend anyway."* Eschewal closes his eyes, and a passage from the black book filters through his mind.

*One must learn to love oneself and realize no perfect person exists who you need to live up to. Love can be found anywhere and any time. When you see it you must cease the moment.*

The words from the black book dispel Eschewal's rationalisations and wash away his fear. He turns back around to make his move on his dream. Disappointment pulls the corners of Eschewal's mouth towards his chin; the girl has vanished. Eschewal steps a few paces forward trying to look through the crowd to spot where the girl has gone. He can't see her, his heart sinks towards his feet.

Eschewal turns back towards Deuce, his mind spinning. He wants to get away and look for the girl but he's embarrassed to come out and say he's no longer a player. Besides he knows Deuce will only laugh at him and say something negative like: *"Come on, bruv, don't run down no girl. Don't be a dick-head be a player, man."*

Eschewal's mind is now working over time to find an excuse to slip away from Deuce, when suddenly three sweet boys, who all greet Deuce, interrupt his thinking. Deuce doesn't introduce Eschewal, so Eschewal says: "Hey, bruv, I'll be back in a minute, yeah."

Deuce nods his head as Eschewal slips away smoothly into the crowd.

# Chapter Twelve

**AS ESCHEWAL STOPS BY** a bridge which leads outside of the park, he begins to beat himself up: *"Why did I take so long to step to her, after all she was going to be my wife? I had nothing to fear."* Eschewal closes his eyes and even though the sun is blazing he feels as if heavy lead-like rain is pelting down on him, drowning him in sorrow. Eschewal opens his eyes, wishing a miracle would float the girl past him but all he sees is a swarm of colorfully dressed people scrambling out of the park.

Eschewal dwells: *'I wonder what ends she comes from?'* He rubs his chin. *'Does she even come from the ends or even from the country? She must come from the ends.'*

He takes out his phone and calls Deuce as he walks back to his car. He tells Deuce to meet him there.

It isn't long before Deuce gets to the car, with a big smile on his face. "Hey, blud, I just got one fit ting you know, bruv. Oh shit, she's hectic, one young ting."

Eschewal is unable to hide his uninterest. "Yeah, true stories, yeah?" he says bluntly.

Deuce notices and questions: "What's wrong with

you, blud? Where did you go anyway?"

"Um," begins Eschewal trying to think what to say, "I went piss init." Smoothly his player dialogue rolls out, "then I saw one ting."

Deuce questions: "What ting?"

"One ting, one old ting, init."

"What, you gonna link her?"

"Nah, nah it's long. Come we go, man."

Eschewal clicks open the car doors, he and Deuce jump in. Eschewal starts the engine. Deuce hits him on the shoulder. "Oi, let's drive around for a bit and see if we can pick up some jezzys."

Eschewal pauses with his response, he remembers:

*To give up on searching for love is like giving up on life. One must never stop until one finds that romantic love partner.*

Eschewal looks over at Deuce, he hates acting like a player but Deuce is his only friend who goes out raving and Eschewal feels that going to raves is the only chance to see the girl again. Eschewal's embarrassment will not allow him to tell Deuce about his pursuit. Instead he will pretend to be a player while he hangs with Deuce and the moment he finds the girl he will end the friendship.

Eschewal nods his head. He puts the car up into gear as thoughts of finding this girl and becoming the creator of values sting through his mind. To be real, he no longer cares to become a creator of values because he feels this girl alone will give him the love and happiness he has been longing for.

# PART TWO

PART TWO

# SIX MONTHS LATER

# Chapter Thirteen

IT'S FRIDAY AFTERNOON. ESCHEWAL sits at his desk looking pissed. He has spent half his wages buying new clothes and attending every rave he could get to and still no sign of the girl in the park.

Eschewal looks up from his screen. You can see the melancholy in his eyes. Behind them, deep within Eschewal's subconscious, doubt has begun chipping away at the persistence it takes to keep on looking for the girl. Slowly a smile stretches across Eschewal's face, as desire consumes him. It's overwhelming, it will not let him stop. He has to find her. He still feels she's going to be his wife and provide him with the happiness he has been longing for.

Eschewal closes his eyes. His latest dream of him and her sailing towards the sun as they exchange vows, emerges clear in his mind, crisp and indestructible. Eschewal opens his eyes and stares ahead.

The voice of one of Eschewal's colleagues snaps him out of his trance.

"I've tried it already, no matter how long you stare at it, it won't go any faster."

Eschewal looks towards his colleague and laughs, now he really wishes the time would tick faster so he could get out of the office and hit the circuit of wine bars and clubs and fulfill his dream.

This thought brings Deuce to mind. Eschewal wishes he had someone else to roll with because it's getting harder and harder to pretend to be a player and still explain why he is not chirpsing any girls. Also Eschewal has to constantly find ways of making the girls, who Deuce pushes on him, not like him. Up to now, Eschewal has been successful in not sleeping with any of the girls but tension is brewing because Deuce is beginning to feel used. Eschewal senses it but has to stick to his plan. He will not sleep with anyone because he wants to be fresh for when he finds his princess. Eschewal thinks he'll be a second time virgin once he has sex with his princess on their honeymoon night.

Eschewal smiles, looks up at the clock. The time reads five past five; fifty-five minutes left. Eschewal blows out hot air. He decides to call Deuce.

Deuce answers the call. Eschewal leans back in his chair. "Yes, sir, what's going on?… Yeah, but what's going on, tonight?"

# Chapter Fourteen

**ESCHEWAL PULLS HIS CAR** around the corner and parks close to the curb. He beeps the horn twice to let Deuce know he's arrived. Ten minutes later Deuce steps out of his door and slowly bops to Eschewal's car. He pops the door and jumps in, Eschewal turns down the music. The men greet.

"Wah gwan, blud?"

"Yeah, wah gwan?" The men hit fists.

Eschewal puts the car into reverse gear then drives towards some type of launch party up in the city. Deuce leans back in the chair, winds down the window then looks at Eschewal and starts a conversation.

"Hey, blud you know how much gyal, is gonna be at this ting?"

Eschewal turns a left onto the main road, and then replies with a smile: "Yeah, true stories, yeah?"

"Course, blud, ber gyal. I'm telling you, bruv..." Before Deuce can finish his sentence he spots two fine young females walking.

"Oi, bruv, stop, stop," he points at the two young females. "Look at that over there, blud. Stop the car, let me spit to them."

Eschewal pulls the car over to the left then swings it around into a U-turn and drives towards the young females. As he stops the car beside them, Deuce jumps out the car and begins his rap. He never usually does this but wants to make a point that he's the one doing all the work to get links.

Deuce jumps back into the car, laughing. "Yeah, blud, those young tings are on it, they said they're gonna link man on the rebound."

Eschewal nods his head and spins the car back around. Before he can put the car into second gear, Deuce spots another two girls. He tells Eschewal to stop. Deuce hollers out of the window to the sexiest one out of the two: "What's going on, babes?"

The girl pushes up her nose, ignores Deuce and walks on with stushness in her step. Deuce feels gutted that the girl blew him out, so he retaliates with a diss: "Jog on, your lip long like liver."

Eschewal begins to laugh. Deuce feels a bit better, his arrogance returns. "You get me doh, blud, she try go on like she's nice for man. With her cheap shoes, come, man, blow."

Eschewal puts the car into gear, turns up the music then pulls away from the curb. He shoots past the 'stush girls' in second gear and onwards to the launch party.

# Chapter Fifteen

**THE STREET LIGHTS ARE** a bit brighter as Eschewal enters into the city's uptown. Most of the shops are still open and the streets are packed with people, making it seem as if it's midday and not nearly midnight.

Eschewal looks at Deuce and decides to start a girl conversation to make him think he is still on his wavelength. "Oi, bruv, do you know one chick name, hold on… I can't even remember her name." Eschewal makes up a name, he still can't remember the name of the girl who he picked up from the bus stop. "Yeah, yeah, Reanne?"

Deuce shakes his head. "Nah, where's she from?"

"I don't even know, I think she's from the ends still."

Deuce scratches his chin. "Yeah, what about her anyway?"

"Nah, I must've linked her one time, init," Eschewal shakes his head. "I swear down, bruv she was stinking — ponging. Ter, but you know what? I was scared to tell her, rudeboy. I just held my nose and pushed it in."

Deuce begins to laugh. "Wait there. What, was she

fit?"

Eschewal shrugs his shoulders. "Nah, not really."

Deuce shakes his head. "Rah, you're selling, if she weren't fit that's long. Listen, the only way I would brush a ting that's stinking is if she's fit and only then she will only be a one pop." Deuce sucks his teeth. "Trust me when I get them butters who are stinking I don't ramp to run dem out of my yard." Deuce sucks on his teeth again. "I tell them straight, 'cause how I see it, I'm doing them a favor, 'cause when they sleep with the next man they will make sure they wash their pussy until it smells like freshwater pussy."

Eschewal begins to laugh. "What's freshwater pussy, blud?"

Deuce looks surprised. "What, don't you know, bruv, that when a girl washes her pussy proper it should be smelling like freshwater." Deuce huffs and continues: "Trust me, that's why I do the finger test, I always do it and if I take my finger out and it isn't smelling like freshwater." Deuce sucks on his teeth once more. "Like I said if she's fit it's a one pop, if she's a butters I don't stop run dem, it's nothing long. Trust me, bruv, certain chicks all they do is wipe out their armpit and spray on deodorant then run outta road and wanna jump in man's bed, and talk 'bout let's get down and dirty." Deuce shakes his head and wipes the corners of his mouth. "It's not that type of party." Deuce looks towards Eschewal with his face screwed and says: "Anyway, how come it's only now you're telling me about this link?" Deuce points his finger. "But you know what, your bad-mind, doh. You know you ain't link me with nothing since we've been moving."

Eschewal now regrets he started the conversation. He uses a lie to slip out of Deuce's valid point. "Just cool, man, I'm gonna link you with something soon man, just cool."

With the sound of a threat in his voice, Deuce says: "Yeah, you better link man with something soon, bruv."

Eschewal doesn't reply as he pushes the car, just in time, before the traffic lights turn red.

# Chapter Sixteen

**ESCHEWAL HAS NOW REACHED** outside the venue and is cruising past the long line filled with girls. The girls come in all shapes and sizes, some dressed in high heels and short skirts, others in low heels and short skirts but all have goose pimples on their legs.

Deuce is talking on his phone. He pulls it away from his mouth and points towards the long line of girls, he whispers: "You see how much girl is here, blud?"

Eschewal nods his head, takes the first left, and begins to look for a parking space.

Deuce ends his call and repeats his last sentence. Eschewal replies: "I see it, blud, I see it, ber gyal."

Deuce hits the dashboard, gassing. "Forget 'bout dat, you know the ting I was just talking too, said she wants to get chopped by two man."

In an unconcerned manner Eschewal replies: "Yeah… is that how she's going on? Better dat," hoping that Deuce will sense that he is not interested in another one of his threesomes.

Deuce gets into gear to convince Eschewal that this

time won't be like the last time. He wipes the corner of his mouth and begins: "Nah I'm telling you, blud, I told her that I'm gonna come down tonight with a friend, init, that's you, init and deal with her case."

Eschewal finds a parking space and rolls his car into it. He looks at Deuce from the corner of his eye and says: "That's long, man. Doing a battery is long, look what happen last time. I swear if that girl ever saw my face, we would be in jail now for rape."

Deuce's right eye twitches and fires back retaliation to Eschewal's resistance. "Naaaaah, it's different this time, blud. This girl is down, she wants to slam two man. What, didn't you hear me talking to her?" Deuce doesn't wait for Eschewal's reply, he quickly adds: "Trust me, rudeboy, this ting is a big jezz, ber man's wet her, fit as well, blud. If you ever see how fit she is, you'll go mad."

Eschewal turns off the engine and remains quiet. He's looking straight ahead, he's lost for words as he struggles to find an excuse. Deuce believes he has done enough to influence Eschewal. He smirks and questions: "So what, you down then, yeah?"

Eschewal pops open the door and replies: "Yeah, man, whatever, man, I'm down." He shakes his head hoping he can end his player pretence soon.

Deuce jumps out of his door and says: "Alright, I'm gonna call her back and tell her we're coming tonight."

The men slam the car doors and make their way back towards the venue.

# Chapter Seventeen

**THE VENUE IS FRESH,** modern and classy looking. Eschewal and Deuce walk past the long line of girls and head for the VIP entrance. Eschewal feels like a celebrity as the bouncer opens the red rope for him and Deuce to enter. Eschewal glances over his shoulder just before he steps through the open glass doors, at the line of girls. Excitement begins to bubble up inside him. He feels sure he will see that girl from the park tonight, because everybody that raves seems to be here tonight.

Deuce gives his name to the pretty woman working the guest list. She ticks him off, plus one. Eschewal and Deuce ascend the marble staircase, which leads to the party. The moment the men enter the party room their eardrums become deafened by music that makes you wanna dance. People surround the bar waiting to be served, others mingle in small groups around different sections of the room.

Deuce taps Eschewal and points towards the bar. The men step over in its direction but, before they can get there, a tall, fresh-faced, well-groomed male stops

Deuce. Everything about this man's appearance seems flashy; from the style of his outfit to his watch and the shoes that he wears. He smiles a broad smile showing large straight teeth, and welcomes Deuce with a hug. They chat for a moment or two. Deuce then turns to Eschewal. "Oi, you know Spiv, init?"

"Course, man, from the ends," Eschewal greets Spiv with a handshake and says: "Yeah, wah gwan, bruv, you safe?"

Spiv replies with a firm nod, but Eschewal doesn't notice that Spiv's eyes hold a glint of coldness. This is due to Eschewal being the younger brother of a person who used to bully and rob Spiv back in the day.

With a forced smile, Spiv turns to Deuce, looks back at Eschewal, nods his head then says: "Alright, peace," and continues walking wherever he was going.

# Chapter Eighteen

**AFTER BEING SERVED AT** the bar, Eschewal follows Deuce over to a corner near the female toilets. Eschewal hadn't realized why, the first time Deuce had led him over to the female toilets, when they began moving six months ago, but now it all makes sense. Eschewal's eyes widen as a stream of girls from outside begin to come in and make their way over to the toilets. Eschewal's heart starts to beat a little faster, butterflies swim in his stomach as two stunning girls walk his way. His heart slows down. He had thought that one of them was the girl in the park. As the girls enter the toilets another wannabe player tries to pull one of them, but she pulls off his grip and enters the toilets with attitude.

Deuce grins. He knows that wannabe player made a fateful mistake. He feels like giving him this advice: *"You need to fall back, player. Never try to pull a female before she can check on herself. You need to relax and wait patiently until she exits, then make your move, gee."*

Before the two stunners leave the toilets, two other groups of girls enter, all looking so fresh and so clean.

Deuce's penis rises. He tries to calm himself but it's no good, he is like a child in a sweetie shop. The two stunners exit the toilets and walk back towards Eschewal and Deuce with eyes fixed straight ahead. Before the one in front can get to walk past, Deuce, he grabs down on her arm. She stops and smiles. Deuce pulls her towards him and begins his rap. Eschewal looks at the friend she is almost as pretty as the girl in the park but just doesn't have that special thing.

Eschewal looks over at Deuce. He knows Deuce needs his help because at any moment he feels the friend will feel left out and end up pulling the girl away from Deuce. Eschewal takes a deep breath and steps to the girl. "So what's your name?" he says in a disinterested tone. The girl answers with a tone of voice that suggests: *don't do me any favors.*

Eschewal replies: "Sorry, what did you say your name was?"

She rolls the lie smoothly off her tongue again, "Leasha."

"Leasha, yeah? That's a pretty name," Eschewal goes for a handshake and introduces himself. The girl smiles and gives him eye contact. Eschewal senses the girl might be contemplating giving him a chance. He can't risk that so he dives in and says: "So what, can I get your number, then?"

Easily, like it's nothing, the girl replies: "I don't give out my number."

Eschewal bites down on his lip. He pretends to lose his voice for a second; he has read the girl correctly. She is a type of girl who has to be talked to with manners and if you're asking for her number you have to do it with much more decorum.

Eschewal plies on the acting. He screws up his face and questions: "Why?"

With another lie, the girl answers: "Cause I've got a boyfriend, init."

Eschewal smiles and fires back with a mind game question: "So how many boyfriends you got, then?" he says with an unconcerned smile.

The girl replies, with a hint of puzzlement in her voice: "Only one."

Eschewal raises his eyebrows. "Is that all?" He then quickly follows up with: "So what, is there no room for one more?"

The girl flicks her neck. "Nah, sorry I'm happy," and as Deuce finishes putting her friend's number in his phone she grabs her friend's arm and disappears into the crowd.

Deuce turns to Eschewal and says: "What did you get her number?"

Eschewal shakes his head and says: "Nah, she was going on stush," then smiles slightly, happy he avoided another possible distraction.

Eschewal closes his eyes for a moment and thinks how many more girls he has to blow out before he sees the girl in the park again. Eschewal shoots his eyes back open as Deuce pokes him in the arm. Deuce is about to give Eschewal another one of his pep talks on playing the game.

Deuce wipes the corner of his mouth. "Listen, bruv," he begins, "for man like you yeah, you need to tell them pretty girls a bling, you get me? You have to become mister bling with them, you get me?"

Deuce takes a sip of his drink and continues. "Tell them something like, you're a promoter and wanna add them to your guest list. Then ring them and give them some other chat, take them out for lunch and talk more shit on a business level and before you know it, you're in their knickers."

Eschewal slightly rolls his eyes and just nods his head as Deuce continues his pep talk.

# Chapter Nineteen

**ESCHEWAL AND DEUCE ARE** now outside in the cold fresh air, which hits Eschewal from all directions. It feels good on his skin. He breathes heavily, in and out, giving his lungs the fresh air they need after being trapped in a smoked out environment for over three hours.

A pretty girl with a tiny head, short hair, tall and slim walks past Deuce and Eschewal. Deuce hits Eschewal on the shoulder and begins to laugh. "Oi you see that girl, yeah?" He doesn't wait for Eschewal to reply. "Listen, cuz, she's some materialistic bitch. Try not link me back when I told her I wasn't driving. All try not even answer my call, bruv."

Deuce's mouth corners turns down into a screw at the thought of the girl seeing his number and just letting it ring. Deuce continues: "Yeah, blud, she try take man for fool, until she saw me in my new ride. Then she start ringing off my phone. Yeah I linked her then sexed her in my car and that was it, never linked her back again or answered her calls."

Deuce begins to laugh. "Yeah, little bitch."

Eschewal throws his car keys in the air and catches them. "Seen, I hear that, bruv. Certain girls love to play too much games."

Eschewal and Deuce cross over the road that leads to where Eschewal parked his car.

Deuce carries on talking. "I'm glad you know that, blud, and you due to know that you can't make them drag you in their sick game. You have to have a tight lid on your emotions, blud. Because you know how many times I wanted to text her a nasty message? Anyhow I did that, bruv," Deuce shakes his head, "I would have never got to wet her, you get me?"

Eschewal nods and says: "True stories."

Both men fall quiet. As they reach the car Deuce receives a text. It's from a girl who he's been linking for the past six months but hasn't managed to sex yet. Deuce hopes that she may be ready to give it up now. So he forgets about the girl who wants a threesome and decides he can't pass up this opportunity. Deuce puts his phone in his pocket and jumps in the car with Eschewal.

# Chapter Twenty

**AS ESCHEWAL STICKS THE** clutch, Deuce sends a message back to the girl; he tells her to call him. Within thirty seconds, she calls back, Deuce answers. "Yeah, what's up babes...? Yeah I'm still coming...? Where do you live again? Alright, darling, I'll be there in about half an hour."

Deuce huffs slightly. He now must play this girl off as the girl who wants the orgy, which is a risk because she might not give him any sex when she sees he's brought a friend. Deuce doesn't care because he feels his game is tight enough to sweet the girl up either way.

Deuce's eyes look worried. He wonders if Eschewal will think the girl's house is too far to travel to. He tells Eschewal.

Eschewal replies: "Blud, I never know she live way over there, dat's far, bruv." Eschewal shakes his head, happy that he now has a good angle to escape another distraction from his goal. "Cuz, trust me, that's long. I'm not even feeling dat, bro. And then man have to drive back afterwards."

Tension runs through Deuce; you can hear it in his voice. "Arh, come on, bruv don't sell it, man's gonna sex pussy you know."

Those words awaken the dog. Eschewal has not sexed for such a long time, but he controls the dog's urges with the thought of the girl in the park. The memory of the girl floods Eschewal's mind. He visualises her good teeth, pretty hands and feet.

Deuce feels that Eschewal is fighting with his mental "demons" and dives in with his hard sell.

"Come on, man, if you ever see how fit this girl is, you know it's gonna be worth it, blud. Trust me, I'm not even lying, she's got some big tits with a cock bottom and on top of that, she's det, blud. Content, she's a sort."

Eschewal shakes his head, pumps the brakes and stops in front of an all-night off license.

"Boy I don't know, bruv. I don't even feel for it." Eschewal pauses, then uses his best excuse. "Because, look what happen last time, you think I wanna go jail for rape? It's long."

"What did I tell you, blud? It's not like that this time. The girl is down, trust me." Deuce dips into his pocket, takes out his phone, and flicks to the message from the girl who wants the orgy. "Look, blud," he shows Eschewal the message, which reads: IF UR FRIEND LOOKS AS GOOD AS U THEN WE CAN SEX.

"Listen, bruv," begins Deuce, in a more confident voice. "I'll even drive back." As he ends that sentence his phone begins to ring. It's the girl who wants the orgy but he plays off as if it's the pretty girl with the small head. "You see, it's that idiot ting we just saw." Deuce ends the call. A few seconds later his phone rings again. "Arh, suck yourself," he shouts to the phone and lets it ring out. He turns to Eschewal and says: "So what you saying, blud, you down?"

Eschewal nods his head in defeat. Deuce jumps out the car, he runs into the off license to buy condoms and alcohol. He quickly returns and Eschewal smoothly sticks the clutch and once more heads for another night of escaping a sexual situation.

# Chapter Twenty-One

**THE WALK TOWARDS THE** girl's front door has Eschewal feeling like he's floating; as if he's experiencing some sort of out-of-body sensation. He begins to think of ways to sour the surroundings once he is up in the house. Maybe he just won't talk or answer any questions.

Before he can decide what to do, the girl answers the door. Straight away he knows she is not expecting to see someone with Deuce. Her eyes look towards him with a hint of coldness. The girl cannot believe that Deuce has taken this liberty and brought another man to her yard. A chill comes over her; she thinks Deuce must have found out about her past. Anger storms through the girl, while images of her having a three-some flash in her mind. The girl feels like spitting, as she remembers sticking her tongue in the anus of the guy she was giving oral sex too. The taste of bottom fills her memory and the hate she felt for herself at that moment while giving that man a batty wash, pours out of her as she looks into the sex-mad eyes of Deuce.

The girl feels like crying. She had hoped that Deuce

might be interested in having a serious relationship with her. "*Bastard,*" she says underneath her breath. "*If it's a battery that you want, that's what you're gonna get, along with a rape charge.*"

Cunningly, the girl slips into acting mode. She releases a smile on to her pretty lips and removes the coldness within her eyes and says: "So what, aren't you coming in?"

Deuce steps up a step and retorts: "Yeah, of course. I was just waiting for you to invite me in."

The girl looks over at Eschewal and says to Deuce: "So who's your friend, then?"

Deuce turns to Eschewal then looks back at the girl. "Oh that's my breddrin, Eros. Oi come, blud," orders Deuce.

Eschewal nods towards the girl and walks up the six steps behind Deuce then enters the house. The girl shuts the door and directs them towards the sitting room; planning to make them pay for all the 'sins' she has been subjected to by the previous men in her life.

# Chapter Twenty-Two

**THE SITTING ROOM IS** neat and tidy. Deuce and Eschewal sit down on the blue leather sofa. The girl has not yet entered the sitting room. She is outside the door listening to Eschewal and Deuce's plan. Deuce says in a high whisper: "Listen, blud, this is what we're gonna do. Give her some drink and put it on her, because at the end of the day even though she wants to do it she might still be a bit boomee, you get me? We got to convince her."

Eschewal looks at Deuce with vexation on his face. "Hold on, bruv. I thought you said she was down? If she's down we don't have to convince her of nothing."

Deuce sits back in the chair and replies philosophically: "Check it yeah, if someone walks into a sweetie shop and comes across ber new sweets they've never tasted before, it's up to the shopkeeper to convince that person that the sweets taste good and are worth buying. If the shopkeeper fails to convince that person, the person will just walk out of the shop without buying nothing. You get me? We are the shopkeepers and it's up to us to convince her to give us her pussy."

Eschewal scratches his head then shakes it from side to side, sucks on his teeth and sits back in the chair. "Yeah, whatever, blud, whatever."

The sitting room door opens. The girl walks in sexily with three glasses. Under the brightness of the light bulb, her full beauty shines. Eschewal didn't realize how beautiful she really is; the girl is stunning and on top of that, her body could beat most bodies belonging to famous superstars.

Cold chills run down Eschewal's spine, as he sees in her eyes what seems like a cunning plan. He can't place it, so he shrugs it off.

The girl takes a seat on the single sofa opposite Eschewal and Deuce and puts down the glasses, then says, as she licks her lips: "What, do you lot bun greens?"

Deuce and Eschewal shake their heads. Deuce says: "Nah, but we got drink, init." Deuce reaches for the bottle of brandy and begins to pour it in the glasses. The girl watches as Deuce pours, she really wanted them to be smokers as well, for it would look even better to a judge and jury that they also came with drugs. 'Not to worry,' she thinks. 'The alcohol should be enough to convict a pair of low lifes.'

Within the next half hour the girl has licked back more than half of the bottle. She seems drunk but at the same time in control of what she is saying and doing. Eschewal has not touched his glass and just sits there listening to Deuce talking a bag of rubbish.

Deuce stands up and smoothly says: "Come, babes. Let me talk to you outside."

The girl giggles and says: "I hope you've got something good to say to me."

Deuce pulls her up and leads her outside.

# Chapter Twenty-Three

**ESCHEWAL IS LEFT IN** the sitting room contemplating how to dodge yet another sexual situation. Deuce has the girl in the bathroom but things are not going his way. The girl has sobered up enough to execute her plan of making Deuce force himself on her. Deuce says: "Why you going on like you don't want sex?"

The girl says: "I do want sex."

Deuce smiles. "So let me hit then, init."

The girl grins. "Nooooo," she says while pushing Deuce away.

Deuce sucks his teeth. "Stop going on silly, man," he says while stepping back to her. Deuce grips her around her waist and bites down on her neck, she moans.

Deuce whispers in the girl's ear: "I know what you want, you want a threesome, init?"

The girl smiles, then pauses in her thoughts and remembers her wild days. It made her sick to think of them, but it seemed that they would always haunt her. *'Why can't people believe that people can change their spots?'* wonders the girl. All she wants in life now is to have a serious relationship. She feels like crying; her inner emotions are all torn up. The girl swallows and answers: "Yeah maybe."

Deuce's eyes show surprise. He expected her to say no, then he would have asked her: *"Would you like to try?"* Instead he says: "So do you want me to call bred-drin?"

With a cheeky giggle she replies: "Yeah, if you want."

Deuce puts his hand underneath the girl's skirt. "Okay in a minute, let me take a quick feel first."

The girl begins to laugh and pulls Deuce's hand out. "What, aren't you gonna call your breddrin?"

Deuce licks his lips. "Yeah, but let me hit it first, man."

The dog jumps on Deuce's back and in a hurry he pulls his penis out, but before he can roll on a condom his semen spits out all over him.

"Shit, what aren't you gonna put it in?" asks the girl, as she licks her lips and rubs her clitoris.

Deuce clears his throat. "I have to get a condom, hold on. I'm gonna call my breddrin as well."

Deuce exits the bathroom and bursts into the sitting room, sweating.

Eschewal looks up. "What, did you hit it?"

Deuce replies: "Course, bro, she got the tight-gripper. Listen, she's in the bathroom waiting for you."

Eschewal hesitates before he gets up. Deuce says: "What, get up then, don't you want any pussy?"

Eschewal doesn't reply, he slowly exits the room

leaving Deuce to clean himself off.

# Chapter Twenty-Four

**ESCHEWAL CALMS HIS HEART** rate as he steps into the bathroom. His body is crying out for sex. The sight of the girl sitting on the sink with her legs spread meets Eschewal's eyes. He blinks, as the dog begins to scream. "Shit!" he says silently as he steps further into the bathroom.

In a low tone, the girl says: "So it's your turn to take me now, yeah?"

Eschewal freezes and slowly replies: "Not if you don't want me to. You don't, do you?"

The girl shakes her head and whispers something that sounds like, "No."

The weight of the dog falls off Eschewal's shoulders. "Alright," begins Eschewal as he nods his head, "I understand, you don't even know me. Listen, I'm gonna call Deuce to come back in, yeah?"

Not looking back Eschewal flees the bathroom with much relief, leaving the girl looking puzzled. She is pissed that she is now unable to call rape.

Eschewal walks back into the sitting room. Deuce begins to snigger, then questions: "What, ain't she gonna make you go thru?"

Eschewal lies. "Yeah but I'm just gonna get a condom in the car."

Deuce smiles, then fronts: "Alright. Oi get me one as well, yeah."

Eschewal nods his head. "Yeah, alright, bro. I'll back in a second."

Eschewal hits the pavement and bops to his car. He starts the engine and drives off smoothly, leaving Deuce on the other side of the city.

# Chapter Twenty-Five

**HALF AN HOUR LATER** Eschewal is back on his ends. He is feeling relieved that he was able to control the dog back in the girl's bathroom. If she didn't say: *"So it's your turn to take me now, yeah?"* and made Eschewal feel like her question had something sinister in it, he would have sexed her.

Eschewal looks into his rear view mirror, his reflection shows a man who looks like he's about to be beaten by the dog in him. Eschewal shakes his head and thinks: *'This task, this goal, it's too big for me.'* He feels that the next situation he encounters, the dog may win. As the feeling leaves him and he turns off the main road taking a sharp left, coming towards him is the corruption of the rotten core of the city. His eyes meet with the corruption, the dog raises its ugly head and begins to scream. Eschewal grits his teeth and continues driving. His eyes dart into the rear view mirror. Quick as a flash the corruption gives Eschewal a faint wave. Eschewal puts his eyes back on the road, and tries to fight this filthy temptation.

Eschewal's eyes again dart back into the rear view,

his foot pumps the brake, the car comes to a halt at the top of the road.

It is too much; the dog has won tonight. His heart pounding, Eschewal begins to reverse to satisfy the dog.

The temptation of corruption begins running up towards Eschewal's car.

Eschewal's insides begin to twist, he starts to hate himself already, for the deed he's about to do, but the dog demands it. He has no control.

Eschewal puts another glance in his rear view. The corruption has stopped running and is walking over to another car.

Eschewal closes his eyes and says: "Thank you." He opens his eyes again and watches as the corruption gets into the car, leaving him alone to face his demons.

Eschewal takes a deep breath and pulls back into the road. He shakes his head knowing he needs to find the girl in the park quickly, before he lets himself slip into the corruption of the world.

# Chapter Twenty-Six

**ESCHEWAL IS SITTING AT** his desk, thoughts of the nasty action he would have done at the weekend exploding in his mind. He wants to slam his fist on the desk and shout: *"WHY!"* but he knows why he lost control, so he relaxes and meditates.

*The key to control destructive behavior is to fill one's life with productive forms of stimulations that outweigh the simulative source that the destructive behavior provides.*

Eschewal slides his finger down his nose and huffs, he knows he is going to be in big trouble if he does not find that girl in the park. She is his only hope to provide a productive source of stimulation that is greater than the dog's urge for promiscuous sex.

A colleague of Eschewal's flips him out of his meditation. "Are you alright, mate?" Eschewal looks up to the voice and dons a false smile. "Yeah, I'm alright. I've just got a few things on my mind."

"Is it anything I can help you with?" enquires Eschewal's colleague.

"Nah, I'm sweet, mate," replies Eschewal with a wink.

The colleague smiles. "Oh I see, women trouble, arh?"

Eschewal nods his head. "Yeah, something like that."

The colleague replies with a nod then continues with whatever he was doing, leaving Eschewal to flip back into his thoughts. Slowly it creeps from the bottom of his heart, sadness spreads itself across Eschewal's face. The dream of him waking up in the morning with the girl in the park as his wife and then dressing their children for school is dissolving each day. Eschewal squeezes his eyes together as he fights back tears. He lowers his head and wipes his eyes. He repeats to himself: *"Be strong, be strong, don't give up, life has to give you what you demand. You will find her."*

Eschewal looks up as his phone begins to vibrate. He looks at the caller ID and it's Deuce, calling him once again to awaken the dog.

Eschewal bites down on his lip and pushes down the anger rising inside of him. The phone stops vibrating and Eschewal receives a message. He listens to it. Deuce offers Eschewal free entry to an exclusive club tonight that only admits the rich and famous, along with a few other lucky riff-raffs.

Eschewal doesn't want to go. He needs to take a break from Deuce, because tempting the dog with all those sexual encounters isn't helping his goal. Eschewal rubs his head, he knows he will be going because he wouldn't forgive himself if he didn't go and the girl in the park had been there.

# Chapter Twenty-Seven

**THE NIGHT STREETS ARE** fresh from a recent downpour. Eschewal is a road away from Deuce's home. He hates raving on a weeknight, but this is the sacrifice he has to take to fulfil his dream. Eschewal stops, parks and waits outside Deuce's house. As usual Deuce makes him wait a while.

Finally, Deuce exits his house then jumps in the car. He brings along a smile and a laugh. He says: "What's up me brudder, everything cool, yeah?"

Eschewal looks towards him and says: "Course man, you dun know," and covers his hand over Deuce's clenched fist. Eschewal pauses for a second waiting to see if Deuce will mention what happened at the weekend. Deuce doesn't and is trying his best not to, so as Eschewal moves through the city towards the club Deuce is biting his tongue from saying: "Oi, bruv, you're a waste-man, you know? How can you leave man on the other side of town? Do you know what I had to do to get home? Not to mention the lies I had to feed my girl. "

Silently Deuce sucks on his teeth and looks through the car window at all the pretty shop fronts whizzing past. Deuce still needs Eschewal as his lift-boy. He will only get rid of Eschewal once his wifey or her people become aware of Eschewal's car. In the meantime, Deuce will plot on how he will get Eschewal back for deserting him.

Deuce looks over at Eschewal then back on the road, as Eschewal turns left along the road leading to the club.

# Chapter Twenty-Eight

AFTER PARKING THE RIDE two streets away, Eschewal and Deuce do a slow walk back to the venue. There is no rush because they would have to wait in the queue regardless whether their names were on the guest list or not.

No more then ten minutes later, they find themselves inside. The first thing about this club, Eschewal notices is the color of the walls and the furniture. They seem to have an effect on the eye which tells the brain to relax and get comfortable. This is exactly what Eschewal does; his state of well-being going into happiness mode.

Deuce taps him on the shoulder and tells Eschewal he'll be back in a moment. Eschewal gives him a smile and a nod. Deuce disappears into the back of the club.

Eschewal steps off towards the bar and from a distance he thinks it's her — the girl in the park. His body feels weak, his palms start to sweat and hairs on the back of his neck stand up.

Eschewal reaches the bar and realises it's not the girl in the park.

A feeling of lust enters Eschewal and he contemplates chirpsing the girl because she has the qualities: the beautiful hands, feet and straight teeth. Eschewal pauses and takes a second to study how she is dressed. His eyes run down her see-though black shirt, which stops just above her belly button. The top four buttons are undone, exposing her cleavage. Eschewal rests his elbow on the bar and watches as the girl begins to dance. She wines up and down with long slender arms above her head. This sexy movement makes her supple breasts move with a life of their own. Eschewal's eyes make contact with her jeans; her slender sexy legs fill them out; designed to turn any red-blooded man on. Eschewal's eyes drop to her open-toe high-heeled shoes, which reveal her beautiful cornless toes. Eschewal nods his head, and in that moment he sees the girl as nothing more than another addictive, destructive drug. The urge of stepping to her disappears, it is replaced with full focus on finding his princess.

Eschewal turns towards the bar and orders an OJ.

# Chapter Twenty-Nine

**IN THE VIP BAR,** on top of the club, Deuce and Spiv are in conversation.

Deuce questions: "Oi, bruv this is big you know. How did you get this link?"

"Didn't I tell you, when I was in pen, I saved my cell-mate from getting robbed, init."

Deuce shakes his head. Spiv continues: "Yeah, two dick-heads from west rolled up in the cell gassed, gassing and try to peel his kettle, init. I just wile them up and run them out the cell." Spiv sips on his drink then continues: "Yeah, it turned out my cell-mate was a millionaire and the watch those pricks tried to suck was given to him by his dad on his deathbed."

Deuce's eyes widen. Spiv continues: "Yeah, true stories, the man was all crying after and thanking me, then promises he will drop some pees on me when I get out, init."

Deuce smiles. "Oh seen. So is this the same man you told me about who owns all these clubs?"

Spiv nods his head. "Yeah, bruv. He owns this one init. He owns hotels and ber clubs. He's even given me a club to manage. So I'll be starting a new weekly club night in a hot minute."

Deuce flicks his head upwards. "Seen, is that how you're going on? Yes, big dog." Deuce hits his fist onto Spiv's fist.

Spiv takes a gulp of his drink and says with coldness in his eyes: "Oi, you know you should stop moving with that teefing yute."

Deuce's eyes show surprise. "Which teefing, yute?"

Spiv points his finger. "Eros init. You shouldn't move with them boy der. I don't trust him and none of his family they're all teefs." The coldness in Spiv's eyes returns as memories of being bullied and robbed by Eschewal's older brother comes to him. But what really burned Spiv was getting his girls stolen by Eschewal's older brother. The breaking point came for Spiv when Eschewal's older brother sexed one of his girls and stretched out her vagina. When Spiv slept with her afterwards he felt the difference, she felt it too and that was the last time Spiv ever felt her. Since then Spiv has had a big insecurity about his penis size. He feels it hasn't grown since he was a little boy and no matter how old he got he still felt like a little boy. He would never make a girl touch him until he had a hard-on and the lights were off. Then immediately after sex, he always made a swift exit to the bathroom to put on extra loose boxer shorts to hide his shriveled up penis.

Spiv bites down on his lip, Deuce leans off the bar and sucks his teeth.

"Yeah, I know he's a cunt, I know he's not safe but I'm just using him as my lift-boy, init. Cause you dun know, man has to be one step ahead of wifey, can't make her spot any chicks in my car, you get me?"

Spiv begins to laugh then gets back to Eschewal. "Oi, you remember how him and his family used to live in that dutty mash down yard? Their yard use to stink, you know."

Deuce cracks up laughing. "Yeah I know, I know, grimy."

Spiv smiles. "Come, man let's go back down to the club."

As the men exit the room, Deuce says to Spiv: "What, blud have you got thru on that chick yet, Manna?"

"Nah, bro. I'm still working on it but as soon as I get it, I'm gonna wok it then dis it for making me wait so long. You know how we do, player."

The men laugh in unison and walk down the stairs.

# Chapter Thirty

**SPIV AND DEUCE ENTER** the dance floor. Deuce spots Eschewal by the bar. Deuce taps Spiv and points out Eschewal. The two make their way over to the bar. Deuce greets Eschewal with: "What's up, bro? What you smiling for?"

For a few seconds the grin disappears from Eschewal's face then returns. He replies: "Its nothing, man, just cool, man, what's going on?"

Deuce shrugs his shoulders. Spiv comes into Eschewal's view, he dons a fake smile. As much as it hurts him he needs to convince Eschewal that he has love for him. He goes into acting mode.

"What you saying, blud?" Spiv rubs his fist on Eschewal's fist then looks at Deuce. "Oi, you know that I know him from long time, init?"

Deuce nods his head. Spiv continues and looks back at Eschewal. "Yeah, man, you're my breddrin, come let me buy you a drink. What you drinking?" Spiv turns to Deuce. "What you drinking, cuz?"

"Anything, man," replies Deuce.

Spiv steps up and leads over to the bar, the attendant moves over to him straight away ignoring the other customers.

Spiv gives over his first two orders, then turns to Eschewal. "Yeah, what do you want, blud?"

Eschewal shakes his head. "Boy, bruv I don't even really drink, cuz."

Spiv retorts: "How you mean, man? Drink something, man. You can't come to the bar and order soft drink. Long, you feel me?"

Eschewal scratches his head, he feels a bit intimidated with the old school peer pressure but remains cool. He flicks his nose and says: "Boy, that's me, bruv, you gotta respect dat."

Spiv laughs, not a disrespectful laugh but a friendlier one, then says: "Just cool, man, show love and drink with the man-dem." Spiv smiles. "Alright listen, I brought some champs. I'm gonna get a box juice, just mix that with the champs then bubble yeah?"

Eschewal can't be bothered to argue so Spiv gets in the drinks.

Spiv begins to spit in Eschewal's ear. He tells Eschewal that he can get him any girl in the club he wants. This is not far from the truth and to prove it, Spiv points out three fit females at the opposite end of the bar. Spiv singles out the fittest one and says to Eschewal: "You know that's content, init? If you want dat, man can link you with dat, you know."

The dog begins barking. Eschewal bites his lip. The girl that Spiv is talking about is hot, but the thought of him fulfilling his dream controls the dog.

The three fit females come over, Eschewal hopes

they will not be feeling what Spiv is saying to them.

Ten minutes later Eschewal finds himself driving over to a penthouse with the three fit females following in tow.

# Chapter Thirty-One

INSIDE ESCHEWAL'S CAR, THE atmosphere is quiet, until Deuce breaks the ice. He says: "Oi, you lot, who's got condoms?" No one answers, Deuce repeats himself: "Oi, ain't you lot got no condoms?"

Eschewal shakes his head then Spiv says: "Just cool, man we deal with that when we get there, man."

Deuce turns towards the back seat and says to Spiv: "How you mean we deal with that when we get there? We need some boots now, blud. It coming like you wanna play with death?"

"Nah, what I'm saying is that room service can bring that."

Deuce turns back in his seat. "Alright, that's what I wanna hear, because there's chicks outta road walking around with disease up their skirt. Trust me, you ever slip with one of these hoes you slide all the way to your grave, you get me?"

No one replies to Deuce's 'words of wisdom.' Deuce then turns the conversation. "Oi, who's taking which one?"

No one says anything, Deuce continues: "Boy I want

the one wearing the short skirt, blud."

Deuce is talking about the fittest girl; he always has to have the best. Spiv grits his teeth, he knows that Deuce will break legs until he gets the best looking girl out of the bunch.

Spiv tries to put Deuce off because he wants to push that girl onto Eschewal. "That ting is on Eros's case, blud, it coming like you didn't see?"

Deuce laughs. "Listen I never see nothing, blud, it's every man for himself. Man's free to make his move, blud, it's nothing."

Deuce looks over at Eschewal. "Oi, bruv, do you want that ting den, yeah?"

Eschewal stops the car at a pair of traffic lights. "Boy whatever, whoever, blud. I'm not bothered," Eschewal lies.

Eschewal's thoughts break as the lights change, he lifts the clutch and moves off.

Spiv says: "Take the next left up there, the hotel is at the end of the road."

Eschewal takes the left. He looks in his rear view mirror to check if the girls are still behind him. They are, so he continues smoothly down the long road.

# Chapter Thirty-Two

**THE GIRLS FOLLOW UP** closely behind, the driver is named Soshana. The one sitting in the passenger seat is called Yashima and the one with the short skirt is named Tanisha. They are all first cousins.

They haven't stopped talking since they left the club. The conversation is now on whom out of Eschewal, Deuce or Spiv has the biggest penis.

Yashima goes first. She begins to laugh as she says: "Nah, nah, I think, yeah. Spiv's got the biggest dick, you know why? I had a boyfriend who was the same height as him and I swear his dick almost reached down to his knee."

Soshana quickly retorts: "Yeah so what? I sexed a guy who was shorter than the other one, what's his name, Deuce, and his dick went past his knee."

Yashima snappily replies: "That doesn't mean his dick was bigger, it could have been the same size or even a bit shorter and just looked longer because it has a shorter way to travel down his leg."

Soshana waves her hand in Yashima's face and says: "Arh your chatting shit, man, init T, ain't she chatting

S?"

Tanisha is brought into the debate. She replies looking very comfortable in the back seat. "Well I don't know, I'm gonna tell you lot this, yeah. I've sexed lots and lots of guys and no matter what their height, their build or looks, their dicks come in all sizes. Like I've had real short skinny guys but when they take out their cocks it's as long and thick as my arm. And then I've had muscular tall men with short skinny dicks and visa versa. So what it's really about is this: some men are blessed with well-built dicks no matter what their body looks like and some men are not. Don't forget you know the dick has muscle in it, and you see how some bres never have to go to the gym to build up their muscles and get them big, the same thing goes for bres with big dicks."

Soshana and Yashima burst out laughing, Yashima says: "So what you saying then girl, men with small dicks can get them big by doing exercise?"

Tanisha wipes the smile off her face and says: "Well it stands to reason, init? If a guy can get the muscles in his arms to grow big by doing exercise he must can get the muscles in his dick to grow big also." Tanisha looks out of the window and smiles to herself. "Anyway, I've heard it's been done and that there is some special dick work-out program that men can do. For real, if you've got a small dick do something about it."

All the girls laugh in unison. Soshana pulls the car over to the curb in front of the hotel. Yashima says: "Alright you lot, who's choosing who, cause I'm saying Spiv."

Soshana chooses Deuce and Tanisha chooses Eschewal, then Yashima says: "Remember how it works, you have to swallow the dick and see how much hand space you have left at the bottom and whoever has the most wins."

Soshana says: "Oi, I hope these guys' dicks ain't cheesy you know? Cause I'm sick and tired of them bres who wanna ask for head and their dicks are cheesy." Soshana curls her top lip. "I'm sure some guys with foreskin don't know they need to pull it back and wash underneath it. Err, long."

Yashima replies: "Nah, my girl if they've got it they pull it back, they're sweet boys, my girl."

Soshana takes the key out of the ignition. "They better be and remember, yeah, whoever loses buys the rounds."

The girls agree and jump out of the car laughing.

# Chapter Thirty-Three

**SPIV AND DEUCE WERE** already out of the car when the girls stop and get out of theirs. They haven't noticed that Eschewal has not got out of the car yet. Eschewal looks into his rear view mirror and sees them joking and laughing with each other. Deuce is already whispering in Tanisha's ear, Spiv tries to distract Tanisha from Deuce but fails.

Eschewal's eyes follow them as they all walk up the stairs towards the doors of the hotel. It seems they don't realize that Eschewal is not with them.

Eschewal thinks to himself that if they all walk through the hotel doors without still realising, he'll count to thirty then blow.

Everyone except Deuce enters the hotel. He stops atop of the stairs and looks down towards the car. He raises his shoulders towards his ears and shouts: "What's going on, fam?"

Eschewal doesn't reply, he pulls the key out of the ignition and pops the door. Deuce walks back down the stairs towards the car.

As Eschewal gets out and shuts the door, Deuce

repeats himself: "What's going on, fam? Aren't you coming up?"

Eschewal pauses before replying. He really wants to say: *"Bruv, I'm not feeling the vibe, I wanna go home,"* but knows Deuce will make him feel guilty by saying: *"Bruv that's bad-mind, why you cock blocking for?"*

So instead Eschewal says: "Yeah, man, I just finish talking to someone on the phone, init. Then I tried to see if I had any condoms in the car, but I haven't got any."

Deuce flicks his fingers towards the floor and says: "Just cool, man, Spiv said we can get some from room service." Deuce turns his head towards the hotel then back to Eschewal. "Come, man," he orders with a laugh, "you going on like you don't want no pussy."

Spiv appears at the hotel door, you can hear the fear in his voice as he says: "Shit, I thought you lot had gone, boy."

Deuce replies: "Nah, man. Everyting is cool, fam. Come let's beat up some pussy."

Deuce leads the way over to the check-in desk and wraps his hand around Tanisha's waist. She does not resist and rubs herself sexily against him.

Soshana and Yashima look at each other and whisper: "She's such a little tart, why can't she play a little hard to get?"

Spiv, without anyone noticing, cuts his eyes at Deuce and then focuses on the concierge. He confirms his reserved penthouse suite which is kept for him two days during the week and one day at the weekend. The concierge hands over the key. Spiv removes the vexation from his face and applies a smile. He knows he won't be able to push Tanisha on Eschewal as he planned. This makes him not even want to go up to the penthouse again. He shakes his head, turns around then shouts: "You lot ready, yeah? Okay let's go and have some fun."

# Chapter Thirty-Four

**EVERYBODY BUNDLES INTO THE** penthouse. Eschewal steps in last. He gently closes the door and slowly walks towards the lounge. Nerves are shooting through Eschewal as he feels there will be no way to escape this sexual situation unless he lets everyone know he has been searching for the girl he saw in the park and doesn't want to have sex with anyone else except her. Eschewal can already hear them laughing and turning his romantic pursuit into something ugly, like stalking. He swallows his nerves and decides that if there is no way out and he ends up sexing one of the girls, he will end his search for the girl in the park.

Eschewal walks into the lounge and gets a surprise; the girls are no longer flirting but are all huddled together on a short sofa. Eschewal looks over at Deuce and Spiv who are sitting on a long curved sofa opposite the girls. He silently mouths: "What, everything flop?" For a moment a smile comes to Eschewal's face, it quickly disappears when he realizes what's happening. The girls are not giving up anything until some money is spent. Spiv knows the drill and gets up from the sofa.

"Come, man, let's get this shit started. What you lot want, champs den, yeah?" Spiv asks the girls.

Tanisha jumps up. "Yeah, that's more like it, I was beginning to think you guys weren't gentlemen," she says with a grin on her face as she follows Spiv over to the phone and rubs his back while he rings room service.

Eschewal looks over at Deuce and it's nothing but vexation on Deuce's face. He thinks Spiv is trying to break his legs, so he decides to try and make Spiv look like a boy.

Deuce leans back into the sofa and shouts to Spiv: "Oi, blud, don't bother ordering the cheap shit ya-na, man's a baller, blud, you get me?"

Spiv ignores Deuce and orders two bottles of the second most expensive champagne on the list and some oysters. Spiv hangs up the phone. "How you mean don't order no cheap shit? Listen, you and Eros better dip into your pockets, 'cause this ain't no freeness."

Neither Eschewal nor Deuce make a comment. Spiv sucks his teeth and scans his eyes over everyone. "Oi, we might as well all get into the Jacuzzi until the champs come."

Spiv doesn't wait for anybody's reply, he holds Tanisha by the waist and walks to the Jacuzzi. As he begins to whisper in Tanisha's ear, Deuce's eyes are burning a jealous hole into his back.

# Chapter Thirty-Five

**THE CHAMPS AND OYSTERS** arrive, the group is half-naked chilling in the swirl pool. Before getting in, Spiv heartily announces to Eschewal and Deuce: "Oi, make sure you lot leave on your boxers you know, 'cause I'm not in no batty man ting." Spiv has quickly drawn card because his penis is not ready for company — for some reason it has shriveled up even smaller than usual.

The atmosphere has changed since the girls got a few drinks down their necks. Spiv has his hand around Tanisha and is talking into her ear. Deuce is still burning with jealousy even though he is touching up Soshana's round perfectly formed breast: maybe too perfect to be real. Yashima is trying her best to get close to Eschewal but it's not quite working.

Spiv looks over at Eschewal from the corner of his eye. He feels it's time to put his plan into action. Spiv had heard previously that Tanisha was carrying some sort of STD and hopes she'll burn Eschewal with it. He pushes himself out of the tub feeling a little more confident that the circulation of warm water has helped to de-shrivel his penis.

Spiv moves over to Yashima and grabs her hand. "Oi, come here let me have a word with you in the bedroom." Yashima does not resist and everyone except Tanisha looks surprised. Sexily, Tanisha paddles over to Eschewal, making Deuce look on in amazement.

Deuce shakes his head and whispers in Soshana's ear and seconds later both get out of the pool and head for the lounge.

Eschewal shuts his eyes as Tanisha begins kissing up on his chest and rubbing him down. Eschewal's penis hardens; the dog begins to bark but he controls himself from touching her back. Tanisha wonders what's up and decides to apply more pressure. She slips her hand into his boxers. Before Eschewal can push her hand away she has his penis. Up and down she goes; fast then slow, gently squeezing the tip. Eschewal closes his eyes and leans back, he begins war with his demons. He thinks all he has to do is slide his hand down to her knickers and pull them off, then they're sexing. Eschewal licks his lips remembering how good sex feels. The dog screams, he feels the urge has won. He silently says: *"Alright, bruv get ready to mash up some pum-pum."*

Then Tanisha says: "I hope you want this like I do?" And just like that the dog jumps off Eschewal's back. Eschewal pushes Tanisha's hand away. Tanisha questions: "What's wrong?"

Eschewal replies: "Can love be bigger than sex? I mean if you truly love something, can that thing stop you from indulging in casual sex?"

Tanisha does not answer. Eschewal pushes himself out the pool, he can feel that power drawing through him. That power of being in love; whether it be achieving his dream or an individual devoting his or her life to religion in exchange for eternal life.

# Chapter Thirty-Six

**NEXT DOOR IN THE** lounge, Deuce cannot believe it. Soshana is playing games! She flicks Deuce's hand away as he tries to guide his penis between the side of her knickers.

"Oi, stop going on silly, man. I thought you was a big girl? So how you going on like you ain't done a one night stand before?"

Soshana blushes and replies: "I am a big girl and I have done one night stands before, but that was before."

Deuce coughs hard, trying to hide his frustration. He shoots back: "So what you saying, you won't do another one?"

Soshana shrugs her shoulders. "I don't know, it depends."

Deuce sucks his teeth. "Depends on what?"

Soshana flicks her hair, "I don't know, the right time."

Deuce huffs, he knows what time it is. He shakes his head and says to himself: *"Please make it be fresh."*

"I know what you want, but I never ever do this."
Deuce kisses Soshana's neck. He thinks: *"Shit, I gotta do this finger test real quick."*

Deuce slides down Soshana's body kissing it on the way. He reaches her belly button and dips his tongue in and out of it and at the same time he pulls her kickers to one side. With his index finger, Deuce goes for the dip. He slides it in and out, making Soshana's juices flow. Deuce looks up. Soshana's eyes are closed. He turns his head to the side and goes for the finger test... it passes. Deuce sucks on his teeth, vexed because he hates having to give head just to get sex, but when his dog is raging, he'll do anything to get it.

Deuce smiles. He gets up from his knees in the darkened room as he prepares to give Soshana the consequences of having to give her oral before sex. He tells her to turn around, then holding his oversized penis he rolls on his emergency condom. (He plans to later cuss Spiv about the unavailability of condoms in the hotel because now he can only do one round.)

Deuce grips Soshana's left shoulder then rams and penetrates. Soshana screams as the pressure from behind bolts though her chest.

# Chapter Thirty-Seven

**IN THE BEDROOM WHERE** Spiv has Yashima, Soshana's screams reach him. The sound alone makes the dog jump on his back. His penis begins to expand even more and with the lights down low, he feels confident to make his move for sex. Spiv looks over at Yashima, she's sprawled over on the bed. He says to her: "So what then, you ready to give me some hairs?" Yashima decides to play games. "Boy I don't know, I don't really get down on the first night you know."

"Ter," says Spiv silently. He smiles over at Yashima, as his semi-hard-on deflates, and says: "Why you going on like that for?"

Yashima does not answer, Spiv repeats: "Come on, man, why you going on like that for? What, is it because I ain't got on no condom?"

Yashima nods her head, Spiv adds: "Arh, just cool, man, you only live once you know, 'cause if you're gonna dead you're gonna dead, it's just your time to go, you feel me?"

Yashima still makes no reply, although she agreed with the last statement, but the condom was not the problem. Yashima also went by the rule that any guy who wants to sex her has to go down on her first.

Spiv sucks on his teeth and gets up and walks towards the door. He pauses in his thoughts, then says: "Come here." He fans Yashima towards him. "Listen to this." Yashima puts her ear to the bedroom door, the sounds from the lounge have turned from screams to a wailing cry that does not reflect pain but an excitable pleasure.

Soshana has by now got used to the size and is enjoying the pounding penetration.

Yashima swallows hard, her nipples stiffen as she hears Soshana now shouting: "Oh shit, you big dick... arh your dick is so big!"

Yashima turns around and hopes that Spiv's penis will be making her say the same words that her cousin is screaming. She kisses Spiv's chest and grabs his buttocks. Spiv leads Yashima over to the bed with a full erection. Yashima makes a grab for Spiv's penis, he tries to pull away but it's too late. Spiv grits his teeth and lets her hold it for a while, then slowly pulling away he hopes she can't really tell that he has a small one.

Spiv turns Yashima backways. He gives her oral for a few minutes then sticks it in and begins to work. Yashima begins to act and gives Spiv a little bit of encouragement with a few cries. Yashima knows it's pointless to do the penis measurement test so she stays bent over until Spiv stops sweating and ejaculates.

# Chapter Thirty-Eight

**THE COLD WINTER SUN** is creeping its way up in the sky, as the guys begin to find their way home.

Deuce smiles, as Eschewal hits the high road that leads to their ends. He grabs his crotch then looks over at Eschewal. "Hey, cuz," he begins, "did you bang your one?"

Eschewal does not take his eyes off the road, he replies: "Nah, blud long, I wasn't even feeling it."

With surprise, Deuce says: "What?! Are you stupid? That fit ting, you didn't kill it?" Deuce looks over at Spiv, lounging in the back seat. "Oi, Spiv," says Deuce, "are you listening?"

Spiv has his eyes closed. "Yeah go on," replies Spiv without opening them.

Deuce laughs and points his thumb towards Eschewal. "Oi you know my man never go thru on the ting doh. Ter, can you believe it that fit blud-clart, ting he never go thru?" Deuce pauses then huffs. "He must've sucked her pussy, fam, you get me?" Deuce laughs to himself at the last statement. He wishes it were true. Spiv makes no reply and keeps his eyes closed.

Deuce looks back over at Eschewal and with a smirk on his face, he questions: "Nah, fam, big and serious, fun and joke dun, did you suck her pussy?"

Eschewal does not crack a smile, he demands: "Hey, bruv, who you talking to, you cat? Oi, bruv you're gassed you know. Oi listen, mind how you talking, you know. How you gonna ask bad man them ting there?"

Deuce flips it on him. "Forget bout bad man, did you suck her pussy?"

Eschewal shakes his head from side to side and changes down a gear, then replies: "Ter, hold on you taking man for some fool? Man don't suck pussy, star."

Deuce fires back: "So what, have you never suck pussy?"

Eschewal looks over at Deuce with his face screwed up. "What, you never hear what I just said: I don't suck pussy, blud." Eschewal puts his eyes back on the road and his mind on the time he went down and tasted hell. Eschewal looks back over at Deuce and feels like spitting. He would never confess to someone like Deuce. Eschewal shakes his head and puts his eyes back on the road.

Deuce knows Eschewal is lying and wishes he wouldn't so he can get his secret out in the open.

Deuce leans back in the chair and sucks on his teeth while Eschewal drives him and Spiv home.

# SIX MONTHS LATER

# Chapter Thirty-Nine

**ESCHEWAL AND DEUCE SIT** in silence with music humming in the background. Not yet has a potential link passed by the car. A few months ago Eschewal had decided that hanging out on street corners could raise his chances of seeing the girl in the park.

Eschewal looks out his car window and his stomach twists, he shakes his head. He has had enough. He wants to give up on his search for the girl in the park, but his heart won't let him. He feels like screaming. He looks over at Deuce. "Oi, rude-boy there's nothing out here," he states with a frustrated tone.

Just before Deuce can retort, a sexy-body girl steps past the car.

"Oh shit, look at that!"

Eschewal twists his head around and claps his eyes on the back of the girl.

Without hesitation, Deuce says: "Rah! I'm gonna call her." Deuce pops the door and springs out. "Oi! Oi-Oi," he shouts. "Oi, baby girl."

The girl takes no notice of Deuce's cry for one reason: her name is not 'Oi.' The girl keeps her head straight and wiggles her way up the road. Deuce shouts for her attention one last time then gives up and spits abuse: "Cha, anyway suck yourself. You're going on like you're nice, like your shit don't stink." Deuce jumps back in the car, his pride dented. He sucks on his teeth. "You see me doh, bruv, try go on like she's nice with her lead-up shoes." Deuce again sucks on his teeth. Eschewal shakes his head and laughs.

Like an actor changing into roles, Deuce wipes the vexation from his face and dons a smile. He winds the window fully down and gets ready to talk. "Hello, hello." He gets the attention from a young-looking girl who is wearing tight-fitted jeans and a low cut top. She stops and turns towards the window.

"What's up pretty, wah gwan?" The girl smiles and moves a bit closer. Deuce sticks his hand out the window and shakes the girl's hand.

"So what's your name then, pretty?"

"Nina," replies the girl.

Deuce nods his head. "Mmmm, Nina yeah, you look good doh, init, Nina? So what, can I get your number?" Nina shakes her head. "Nah, I can't."

"Why, have you got a boyfriend?"

"Yeah, I got a boyfriend, and he wouldn't be too happy with me chatting to next man, init."

Deuce smirks. "Alright, babes. I'm not gonna hold you up no longer, I'm gonna let you go."

A slight disappointment flashes across Nina's face; she wants a bit more attention. She waves, turns on her heels and says: "Bye."

Moments later, Deuce shouts: "Oh shit! Look at them two chicks, blud."

"Where?" says Eschewal, crocking his neck trying to spot the girls.

"Over there, crossing the road."

Eschewal spots the two thick body girls both wearing short skirts.

"Come, man, let's jump out and call them," demands Deuce.

"Hold on, man, wait until they cross the road, man."

Deuce sucks on his teeth. "You're going on like you're frighten," then hops out the car. Eschewal stays seated and watches.

"Oi," bellows Deuce getting the girls' attention just before they can swerve off to the right and walk down the main road. They look towards him, he waves them over. The girls grab each other by the arm and stroll towards Deuce with grins on their faces.

# Chapter Forty

**THE GIRLS WANT TO** work as fast as Deuce with the exchange of numbers and setting a time to link. Eschewal gets out of the car and heads towards the corner shop. Deuce gets the numbers from the girls and watches as they walk off, hoping to make more links.

Eschewal is on his way back from the corner shop, he does not notice a pair of luscious legs behind him. Deuce spots them instantly, he starts to indicate to Eschewal to stop the girl. Eschewal cannot hear what Deuce is saying and keeps on stepping towards the car. He reaches it and opens the door. Deuce shouts and points: "Look, cuz. I was telling you to stop that chick." Eschewal looks around and catches the back view of the girl. He says: "So why didn't you jump out and stop her?"

Deuce sucks his teeth. "Cause you was right near her, init, you dick-head." Deuce pops the car door and makes chase for the girl. He reaches the edge of the corner and hollers at her: "Hello, hello!"

The girl stops and turns around. Deuce waves her to him. She hesitates and squints her eyes as she tries to make out if she knows Deuce.

Deuce waves again. "Come here, man."

Reluctantly the girl strolls up to Deuce with her two shopping bags.

Eschewal watches from the car as Deuce spits his game. The girl smiles and nods, she smiles and nods again then moves off the corner towards the car with Deuce leading.

Deuce gets to the car and says to Eschewal: "Oi, blud, you don't mind to drop this beautiful girl home, do you?"

Before Eschewal can reply, Deuce mouths: "We can link her later and both go thru."

Eschewal wants to say: *"So what, I do not want a three-some, I just want to find the girl in the park."* But he simply shrugs his shoulders and says: "Yeah, whatever, I'll drop her."

Deuce and the girl bundle in, Eschewal drives off.

# Chapter Forty-One

**AS ESCHEWAL DRIVES ALONG** the high street he passes scrolls of people walking, enjoying the summer night. He looks into his rear view mirror and into the eyes of the girl. He catches a glimpse of her lustful, fiery sexual passion. He knew from this that Deuce has spoken the truth and she will be up for a threesome. Suddenly butterflies hit Eschewal's stomach as the dog raises his ugly head. Eschewal thinks: *'Shit, how the hell am I going to control this dog after going without sex for one year?'* Eschewal now smiles as he thinks he will let the dog take over. At least this way his heart hasn't a chance and he will have to end his search as he loses control and does the threesome.

Eschewal pulls the car into a sharp right, shakes his head again, as he reminisces on a sentence from the black book: *One needs the discipline to think. Then comes control.* Silently Eschewal says: "Yeah."

Deuce looks over at Eschewal. "What, did you just say something, bruv?"

"Nah, nah," replies Eschewal as he flicks his nose.

Deuce spins round to face the girl and says loud

enough so Eschewal can hear: "Oh, I thought you asked if this girl was adventurous." Deuce waits for Eschewal's reply hoping that he will follow his lead. With a deep breath Eschewal says: "Nah... why, is she?"

Deuce smiles seductively. "Course she is, ain't you, babes?"

The girl licks her lips. "Well that's for me to know and for you lot to find out, init."

Deuce loves when girls use that phrase; it always gets him aroused. "That's what I keep telling them, ter, she's cold," says Deuce excitedly, then adds: "So what, can we link you later on and find out, then?"

"I don't know, um," begins the girl as she thinks what time her so-called boyfriend (who she hasn't seen for a month) promised he would come around. He told her nine, it was eight now, so she decides to give him an extra hour and if he does not show up she will go off with Deuce and Eschewal. The girl answers Deuce: "Yeah maybe. Take my number and give me a call about ten o'clock."

Deuce nods his head eagerly. "Yeah go on, what's the number."

The girl taps Eschewal's shoulder. "Yeah, babes, stop here."

Eschewal stops the car outside a tall grey housing block. The girl finishes giving Deuce her number. As she gets out the car, Deuce slips his hand between the girl's bum cheeks for a quick feel.

"Naughty," says the girl.

Deuce quickly replies: "Listen, I'm gonna be even

more naughty, when I come for you."

The girl sticks out her tongue and swishes her head forward as Deuce shouts: "Oi, what's your name again?"

"Salacious," says the girl without turning back, leaving Deuce to watch her big bottom moving up and down as she walks to her housing block.

# Chapter Forty-Two

**DEUCE AND ESCHEWAL ARE** making their way over to a wine bar to kill some time until 10 o'clock.

"Oh shit, she's fit," says Deuce as Eschewal connects to the main road.

"Nah, blud serious," begins Deuce, "do you really know how fit that chick is?"

Eschewal bops his head quickly in agreement. "That's what I keep telling them."

Deuce continues: "Ter, can you imagine how her body looks when you take off her clothes? I swear you due to bus a nut before you even push it in."

Eschewal shakes his head and laughs. "Yeah, true stories?" he says.

"Yeah, cuz," says Deuce, "but not me, cause I'm rolling with the fitness, blud. Trust me I'm not busting until I mash that down."

Eschewal smiles. "Yeah, better that boy," then rubs his head.

Silence falls between the two for a short while, then sounding less scared but more concerned, Deuce says: "Oi, you don't think she'll back out do you?"

Eschewal half shrugs his shoulders, "Boy I don't know, bruv," he says, hoping that she won't.

Deuce continues: "Nah, I don't think she's gonna back out. I'm telling you, bruv every girl that I know are hoes, trust me. That's why I do what I do. Even though I love my wifey, I don't trust her, you get me?"

Eschewal raises his eyebrows not in agreement but in understanding Deuce's guilt driven rationalisation. He pushes the car through the last set of traffic lights and drives past the wine bar. As he looks for a parking space his memory replays the look of sexual need in Salacious's eyes. *"Yeah"* he tells himself, she won't be backing out.

# Chapter Forty-Three

**THE TIME IS FIFTEEN** minutes to ten. Salacious has been arguing with her boyfriend for the past hour. Her battery has just died so the arguing is cut off but the argument has not ended. Salacious runs to the charger and plugs in her phone. With tears waiting to burst from her eyes, she waits, until her boyfriend answers the phone.

"Yeah, so what are you saying?"

"You know what I'm saying," replies the boyfriend.

Salacious's throat begins to choke up. "Yeah, but I don't understand, why?"

The boyfriend lowers his tone of voice. "You know why. I need some space. Like the relationship is going too deep too quick."

"What do you mean?" cries Salacious. "We've been seeing each other for over six months. And I haven't even seen you for a month."

"Yeah I know, but you've heard what I've said." Salacious is now crying. The boyfriend overlooks the tears, then says: "Listen, I'm going to talk to you, I'm gonna talk to you soon but I've gotta go, later." The boyfriend ends the call, running the biggest bling that he hopes will leave Salacious psychologically weak for him. The mind game would have worked because even though Salacious is a very beautiful girl and has a nice personality she has low self-esteem. From a little girl her mother told her: *"Why can't you tidy up your room and keep it clean? You know when you get big you're never gonna be able to keep a man because no man don't want no nasty girl who can't clean."*

These taunts haunted Salacious and whenever she had a boyfriend she lived in fear that, somehow, he would see in her that untidy little girl.

Salacious sits on the edge of her bed holding her phone, sobbing. Her phone rings, a foreign number flashes up, she wipes away the tears and answers: "Yeah, hello?"

"Yeah hello, is this Salacious?"

"Yeah, who's this?"

"Ricky," lies Deuce. He continues: "Um, yeah, one of the dudes that dropped you off earlier."

Salacious jumps into her sexy character voice. "Hi, what's up, babes? I didn't think you was gonna call."

"Course I was gonna call," replies Deuce. "So what you saying? Are you going to link man?"

"Um... yeah, um, come and pick me up in about half hour."

Salacious ends the call. She throws down her phone on the bed and runs to the bathroom to freshen up.

# Chapter Forty-Four

**DEUCE SLAPS ESCHEWAL ON** his arm. "Oi, blud, she said we must pick her up in half an hour." Deuce grips his crotch. "Oh shit, we're woking tonight, blud."

Eschewal shows no emotion, he had misjudged his heart. It had beaten the dog back into its cage. It will not let him give up on his dream. "Oi, bruv," he begins, "I'm gonna be real, I'm not even feeling it."

"Feeling, what?!" says Deuce, sounding puzzled.

"Yeah, bruv, I'm not feeling this threesome ting. I'm not on it."

Deuce's voice almost chokes up. "Why?"

"This galist ting is getting long. I want a wifey as well," lies Eschewal. All he wants is a wifey, namely Manna.

Deuce sucks on his teeth. "Having a wifey is long you know. Ber headache, bruv. I wish I was like you with no wifey."

Eschewal huffs, he shakes his head. "Nah, trust me, bruv, I'm not on it. It's long."

Deuce's heart drops, he panics and says: "Oi, bruv,

to find a wifey is hard you know, and trust me you will never find one if you go out looking." Deuce screws his face then continues: "That's what life is like, bruv. When you want something you can't get it and then once you get it you don't want it..." Deuce takes a quick pause to see if he's beginning to sway Eschewal's decision. He continues as he points his finger. "Yeah, so you should just bang different chicks, bruv until you find the one."

Eschewal shakes his head, not knowing how to answer. He has to be careful not to blow his cover that he is not a player anymore.

Deuce falls silent and changes tactic. "Alright, at least let me bring her to your yard then?"

"Nah, bruv laow that, man."

"Arh, go on, man please, man, you know I would do it for you. Come, man please."

Eschewal sucks on his teeth and feels like cursing. "Alright, man but this is the last time you know."

Forty-five minutes later Eschewal pulls up outside Salacious's housing block. Salacious comes out wearing tight jeans that are tucked into high heeled boots and a waist high jacket. She pauses for a few seconds then taking two deep breaths, she makes her way over to Eschewal's car.

# Chapter Forty-Five

**FOR THE PAST FIFTEEN** minutes, Deuce has been trying to get Salacious next door in the bedroom. "Nah, stop!" she says, leaning off Deuce's shoulder.

"Arh, babes, man why you going on like that for?"

Salacious pulls Deuce's hand from behind her. "Just give me some space, man."

Deuce is about to suck his teeth and diss Salacious but holds it down. He smiles then whispers: "So what you saying? You need a drink, before anything go on, init?"

Salacious twiddles her hair. "I'm not saying that, but it would be nice to have a drink, yes."

Deuce looks over at Eschewal and grins. "Oi, blud, I beg you a favor, go shop for me please?"

For a moment Eschewal doesn't respond or take his eyes off the T.V. Slowly he slides his hands down his legs as he stretches them out. "Alright, give me the money then," he says with an even tone. He just wants Deuce and Salacious out of his house as quickly as possible.

Deuce gets up. "Buy me a half-a-bottle of brandy,

yeah." Quickly Deuce mouths: "And a box of condoms."

Eschewal nods his head. "Alright, man, I'll be back in a minute," and leaves the room.

Salacious looks at the time on her phone, she had hoped her boyfriend would have called back deterring her from what she's about to do. Under her breath, she says: "Bastard," then switches off her phone. She turns to Deuce close enough to kiss him and says: "Are you upset with me, babes?"

For a moment Deuce does not answer and wonders: *'Why do girls love to play games, man?'* Deuce shakes his head and smiles. "Nah I'm not upset, babes, but you're going on cold, init?"

Salacious licks her lips. "Um, I just got something on my mind," she says, while pushing her body onto Deuce. Instantly Deuce gets an erection.

"Yeah, well let me try and take that off your mind." Deuce begins to grope Salacious up and down. Salacious lifts up her head, revealing her neck. Deuce bites down on it, Salacious moans. Deuce sucks and licks, Salacious moans some more. Deuce's hand wonders towards her crotch. He undoes the two top buttons and says: "Oi, come let's go next door to the bedroom?"

"Nah, I'm not ready," says Salacious, as she buttons up.

"What?" responds Deuce, sounding confused and upset, for the dog is upon him and needs to unleash.

"Nah, not yet," pleads Salacious as she moves away.

Deuce sucks on his teeth. Thoughts of getting ruff with Salacious come and go because any minute Eschewal could come back.

SEACIEKO

# Chapter Forty-Six

**ESCHEWAL PULLS UP TO** the curb in front of his house. From out of nowhere, a vision hits him. He sees himself and Deuce sexing Salacious, he shakes his head and switches off the engine.

He picks up the brandy and the vision hits him again; harder. He grits his teeth and clicks open the door. As he jumps out, his heart is beating, the vision becomes clearer, the dog is barking.

"Shit," he says as he shuts the car door and locks it. Eschewal blinks his eyes and focuses, he feels like swearing. He can't believe that just one vision has released the dog. He waits a moment to see if his heart will respond... nothing, the dog is loose. Eschewal's only hope is if Deuce has already sexed Salacious, because if he hasn't a threesome is going down; drawing the search for the girl in the park to an end.

Steadily Eschewal approaches his front door. He takes a second to think: *'This world is nuts. It seems as if it only gives you a beautiful wifey, who will love you and do everything for you, only if you plan to give her bun twenty-four-seven.'*

Eschewal shakes his head, pushes his key into the lock, and quietly enters his house. He stops in the passage for a moment and listens if he can hear any sexing. He can't hear any, so he closes the door with a bang just to make sure that if they are sexing they're not anymore.

# Chapter Forty-Seven

**ESCHEWAL ENTERS THE ROOM.** He can't tell if anything went down but as he walks over to hand Deuce the brandy he takes a sniff of the air just to make sure.

Deuce takes the bottle. "Nice one, mate," he says, as he begins to pour Salacious her drink. Deuce looks over at Eschewal who is making his way over to sit down. "Oi, blud, do you want a drink?"

"Nah, I'm cool," replies Eschewal as he sits down.

"What, don't you drink?" questions Salacious.

Eschewal rubs his chin and shakes his head. "Nah, I don't drink."

Salacious looks at Deuce. "So, what, you don't drink either?"

"Nah, babes, I don't really drink, but I'm gonna have a little glass, you get me?"

Salacious smiles, rubs her hand down her leg. "So what, you lot plan is to get me drunk, and have your wicked way with me?"

Smoothly Deuce replies: "Nah, babes. Don't say that. Nothing can't go on if you don't want it to go on.

You feel me?"

Deuce gives Salacious her drink. Hesitantly she takes it with a sexy smirk. She sips the drink then licks her lips. "Ooh, too strong, do you wanna kill me? Nah, eya mix it a bit more."

Deuce dilutes the drink some more until Salacious tells him to stop.

Salacious crosses her legs, smiles then takes a gulp of the drink. Slowly the drink takes effect. Salacious closes her eyes and licks her lips. Her body begins to feel heavy as if gravity is pulling her towards the floor. Like a bolt of electricity, her mind sends chills up and down her spine, her nipples prick up, she's horny.

Salacious gets up from the seat and puts her glass down. Calmly and cool, she says: "Alright guys, when I get back from the bathroom, you lot better be stripped naked and ready, cause I will be."

Eschewal looks at Deuce with an expression that says: *Is she for real?* Deuce raises his eyebrows and shrugs his shoulders.

# Chapter Forty-Eight

**SALACIOUS HAS BEEN IN** the bathroom for five minutes. Deuce gets an idea to go in there after her and finish off what he thought he was about to get before Eschewal came back. Deuce gets up from his seat and walks towards the door, he opens it then quick as a flash he steps back in. "Oh shit," he says as he begins stripping off his clothes.

Looking confused Eschewal says: "Hey, what you doing, blud?"

Deuce swings around, slips his right leg out of the jeans and throws it on the floor. "What do you mean, what am I doing?"

Eschewal retorts: "Ter, what you doing, what you stripping off for?"

Deuce drags off his shirt. "Ter, sick, we're getting pussy tonight, gee."

Eschewal makes no reply, for he now knows Deuce saw something in the hallway. What Deuce saw, not even he expected to see — the silky smooth firm body that lay beneath the clothes that Salacious was wearing. And before Deuce can take off his vest, the door pushes open. In steps Salacious, with perky, erect breasts and wearing silky cream thongs.

Butterflies, probably at the same time, hit Deuce and Eschewal in the stomach. It was rare to see a body like Salacious'. Small waist, a perfectly round juicy bottom and firm supple breast.

With seductive eyes and curling her lips sexily, Salacious says to Eschewal: "What, aren't you getting undressed?"

Before Eschewal can answer, Deuce leads Salacious out of the room. He turns to Eschewal and simply says: "Ter, sick!"

# Chapter Forty-Nine

**ESCHEWAL IS LEFT IN** the sitting room with a full erection and the dog howling. In his mind's eye Eschewal sees the face of the girl in the park and remembers the way she made him feel. The feeling was beyond lust, it consumed him and took his breath away. The feeling could only be love; a love, which is the strongest emotion a human can feel. A love that Eschewal has begun to believe he would never be allowed to have.

It seemed as if Eschewal had blinked his eyes after that last thought and when he reopened them he found himself standing in the bedroom in his boxer shorts, looking down at Salacious. He had hoped before now the girl in the park would have saved him from the dog's urges: he was wrong.

Deuce turns his head to Eschewal. "Oi, bruv," he begins as he lifts Salacious's right leg, exposing her vagina.

"Have you ever seen anything like this? Look how good it looks, bruv."

In the very same moment that Eschewal looks at

Salacious's pretty vagina, he destroys the mental image of the girl in the park.

The search is finally over. The goal not to have sex again until he finds the girl in the park crumbles away as he pulls off his boxers and slips on a condom.

# THREE MONTHS LATER

# Chapter Fifty

**ESCHEWAL AND DEUCE ARE** sitting in a wine bar. Eschewal's face is subdued. He cannot believe the search for the girl in the park is over. He was so sure she was made for him. Eschewal sips on his OJ and rests his eyes on Deuce. For over a year, since Eschewal decided moving with Deuce was a good idea to find the girl in the park, Deuce had linked him with over fifty girls. Every single one, except Salacious, Eschewal had dodged from having sex with.

The feeling of wasted time makes Eschewal feel sick. Eschewal looks away from Deuce. He has made his mind up, he will waste no more time and will not let the dog take over his life. The first female who catches his eye he will make her his wifey; his one and only.

Deuce turns to Eschewal. "Oi, blud, it looks like there's gonna be ber, young tings in here tonight, blud."

Deuce is right, there will be a new set of young females fresh out of college ready to enjoy the freedom of weekend raving.

Eschewal nods then smirks, he would not mind a

young female that he could groom. He sips on his juice then says: "Yeah, it looks like it, init."

Deuce leans back in his chair feeling excited that he has his right hand man back with him, setting out on another rampage; unaware Eschewal has other plans.

Eschewal twists his head slightly to the left, his eyes bring into view a young female by the bar. He studies her for a bit and takes notice of her good teeth, pretty hands and feet. Eschewal begins to imagine himself marrying the girl and making sweet love to her, the vision blurs with the image of the girl in the park. Eschewal huffs and silently repeats: "That dream is over. The dream is dead."

Swiftly Eschewal gets up from his seat and slides over to the bar where the girl stands. Deuce takes a sip of his drink and watches with envy as the girl gives Eschewal her number.

# Chapter Fifty-One

**THE CAR IS MOVING** smoothly through the night streets, music plays in the background. Eschewal slows the car down as he approaches a roundabout and indicates to go right.

"Nah, blud take the left," says Deuce. "I'm hungry, blud, what aren't you hungry?"

"Yeah, I'm kind of hungry still," says Eschewal as he stirs the car left and moves down the road towards an all night fast-food takeaway.

Deuce flicks his fingers towards Eschewal and says: "Oi, bruv, did you get that chick's number?"

Eschewal plays the fool. "Which chick?"

"The chick back at the bar, man. The fit ugly ting."

Eschewal kisses his teeth then replies: "She ain't ugly, why you hating for? Don't hate, the girl is abstract, man."

Deuce rolls his eyes. "Forget bout that, the bitch is ugly, man, but she's rass-clart fit. She's fit till I feel sick. What, did you get the number, then?"

Eschewal pulls the car to the curb in front of the takeaway. His player dialogue rolls out. "Course, man,

I don't ramp you know."

He picks his phone up off the dash and begins to flick through his contact numbers just to check if he has stored the number.

Deuce asks: "Oi, what's her name?"

"She calls herself Peachy."

"What, is that her real name?"

"That's what she said, gee." Eschewal throws the phone back on the dash not realizing what is about to happen to him.

Deuce dips into his pocket. "Arh, bruv, listen I'm tired you know. I beg you get the food for me, please."

Eschewal nods his head, takes Deuce's money and jumps out of the car.

Deuce picks up Eschewal's phone. He plans to steal Peachy from him because back at the bar, just for a split second, Peachy had taken her eyes off Eschewal and placed them on him. At that moment, seeing the lust in her eyes, Deuce knows he can steal her from Eschewal. Smiling, Deuce pulls Peachy's number.

# THREE DAYS LATER

# Chapter Fifty-Two

**ESCHEWAL REACHES FOR THE** T.V remote as the latest top comedy show ends. He flicks through the other channels and finds nothing to watch. The next suitable show will not be starting until the next hour. Eschewal throws down the remote on the stylish coffee table and rests back into his leather sofa. Eschewal stares up at the ceiling, he sighs then shakes his head. He closes and rubs his eyelids then opens them and continues to stare at the ceiling, he thinks on what to do now to kill some time. He smiles as he recalls the phrase. *You do not kill time, time kills you.*

Eschewal sits up and looks over at his phone and for a few seconds he does nothing. Then as if he has received an electric shock, he jumps towards his phone. Eschewal remembers that he has not phoned Peachy yet. Eschewal scrolls down to Peachy's name, resumes a cool composure. He moves over to his CD player and turns on some music.

Eschewal pushes the call button and sends a dialing tone to Peachy's phone. He sits down as it rings. A second later, Peachy answers.

"Yeah, hello," begins Eschewal as he swallows down the rising butterflies. "Is this, um, Peachy?"

"Yeah," says Peachy, "who's this?"

Eschewal relaxes further into the seat as Peachy's welcoming tone puts him at ease. "Oh, what's up, babes? This is um, Eros... we met at the bar last week."

Peachy laughs, a cutie laugh, and says: "Oh yeah, are you all right? What are you up to?"

Eschewal blows out air, then replies: "Um, um just chilling, babes. So what are you saying? When are we going to set a date to get to know each other better?"

"I don't know. It's up to you."

Eschewal smiles that Peachy responds positively and doesn't lead the conversation into a long-ting, because he hasn't got much credit left on his phone. Confidently, Eschewal suggests a movie on Friday at eight. Peachy agrees. Eschewal ends the conversation with a sweet compliment. Peachy smiles then laughs her cutie laugh and says, bye.

Eschewal ends the call and his thoughts drift off as he wonders: *'Is she the one?'*

# Chapter Fifty-Three

**SITTING IN HIS CAR,** moments later, Deuce dials Peachy's number.

Deuce turns down the music from the radio, as Peachy answers her phone.

"Yeah, hello," says Deuce," is this arh, Peachy?"

With suspicion in her voice, Peachy says: "Yeah... who's this?"

Deuce clears his throat. "Yeah um, this is Ricky." A moment of silence passes as Peachy waits for Deuce to continue.

"I don't know if you will remember me, but you gave me your number a few months ago, at that bar on the high road."

Peachy is about to hang up because the only time she has ever been to that bar on the high road was when she met Eschewal and that was three days ago. However, the excitement of discovering whom this mystery caller is makes Peachy stay on the line.

With a little giggle Peachy says: "Is it? Are you sure I gave you my number? Because I hardly ever give it out."

"'Course I'm sure," begins Deuce. "How else did I get your number then?"

Peachy giggles once again. "That's what I want to find out. What did you say your name was again?"

Deuce swallows. "Ricky," he pauses then begins to describe himself. "Don't you remember me? I'm like well-built, short hair and dimples."

Peachy licks her lips as the description resembles the guy she saw with Eschewal. Peachy shakes her head and says: "You know what, I don't remember you. This is a wind up, init?"

Deuce coughs, then panics. He knows if he says the wrong thing, he will lose the chance of linking Peachy. He decides to be upfront and tell Peachy the full hundred.

"Alright," begins Deuce, "I'm gonna be real with you. I saw you at that bar three days ago, and you gave your number to my friend, who had on the blue cap. Well I thought you were so criss I stole your number out his phone and boy I wanna link you."

Peachy becomes light-headed, she had wished that Deuce had spoke to her instead. She makes no resistance as Deuce suggests they meet within the next hour.

Deuce grins. The steal went down easier than he thought. He grips his phone. *Why are these chicks so stupid?* begins Deuce to himself. He continues: *They always want the best-looking dudes, the shotters or the baddest boy on the block but can never handle the harsh consequences.* Deuce shakes his head. *Stupid bitches. Always, looking surprised when they find out they got played.* Deuce huffs: *What do they expect when they link a pretty boy like me?"* Deuce looks into his rearview mirror, slides his tongue over his teeth and says: "Yes, sweet boy, just another hoe."

Deuce puts the car into gear heading off to destroy and demoralise, with his lies and dishonesty, another female soul.

# Chapter Fifty-Four

**DEUCE IS RESTING WITH** his back against the head board. Peachy is in the bathroom. She steps back into the room ready for sexual intercourse. She sits down beside Deuce in an S shape, curls her lips, and says: "I don't know, I feel bad linking you now, after I talked to your friend and gave him my number."

Deuce flicks his nose and replies: "Don't feel bad, babes you done the right thing, trust me. Like he is my breddrin and that, but you listening, he's a dog. You feel me? He's all got a wifey so you done know he's not gonna take you seriously."

Deuce looks down at Peachy. He strokes her hair and stares in her eyes. "Nah, dem boy der don't deserve a beautiful girl like you. You're too good for him, trust me."

Peachy smiles. She wants to believe what Deuce is telling her so her motives can be justified. She leans off her elbows and brings her body to the edge of the bed and questions: "So what about you, haven't you got a girl? Because you know what they say; birds of a feather flock together."

Without cracking a smile, Deuce hits Peachy with the twisted truth: "Yeah, I'm gonna be real, I have got a girl but it's not working out. I've already told her I want to end it but she's still clinging on and right about now I wanna get to know you. Upfront, I'm not saying that I wanna jump into a relationship with you right away but I do want to do a ting with you and just go with the flow."

For a moment, Peachy remains quiet as she dwells on the information Deuce has fed her. The information contains elements of honesty and hope, which are enough to convince Peachy's need for justification that Deuce could be the one that she has been waiting for all her life.

Deuce brings her away from her thoughts as he says: "So what you saying, babes, you wanna go with the flow and see how it goes?"

Peachy licks her lips then shrugs her shoulders and says: "Yeah, alright then, I'm down with that."

For the next hour, Deuce delivers foreplay until he gets Peachy comfortable enough to give him sex.

# Chapter Fifty-Five

**THE BIG DAY FINALLY** arrives. Eschewal has been looking forward to his date with Peachy and is glad the working week has ended.

Eschewal dips his head underneath the bath water then resurfaces and begins to soap himself up. He dips his soaped up body back into the water then rinses off under the shower. Body now feeling fresh and clean, Eschewal brushes his teeth.

He walks into his bedroom, body now dried off, with the towel wrapped around his waist. Eschewal begins creaming himself down with body lotion, he starts from his face all the way to his feet.

Eschewal turns up the volume on the music that is now blasting through his flat. He gives a dance with a wiggle and a turn then stops. He picks up the roll-on deodorant and rolls it under his armpits then between the inside of his thighs. He then picks up the spray deodorant and sprays every nook and cranny. Eschewal steps back. Looking at the expensive eau de toilette he wonders which one out of the six bottles he should wear tonight. He decides to wear the one that makes him smell sweet but not that sweet for it to be mistaken for perfume. Eschewal lays the sweet scent all across his chest in a criss-cross motion then over his head. He moves back towards his bed, where his recently dry-cleaned outfit is laid out, and sprays it with the scent.

The sweet-boy preparations are now complete. The only thing left to do is put on his clothes.

Eschewal looks over at himself in the mirror. He sees his trapped image staring back at him, longing to experience a life of happiness. Eschewal speaks to his image and says: *"As long as I can see you, then I know I still can become happy."* The image makes no reply, just reflects back a sense that it understands. Eschewal turns away and puts on his clothes.

He is now finally ready. He looks at the time. He has half an hour to pick up Peachy and half an hour to get to the cinema. He decides to give Peachy a call and let her know he's on his way. Eschewal activates the number; he puts the phone to his ear and begins to smile, ready to reflect the smile in his voice. The smile slowly disappears from Eschewal's face as the phone rings out. His heart sinks at the reality of what might be happening: that Peachy is listening to the phone ring and not answering it because it has his number flashing on the screen.

Eschewal shrugs off those negative feelings and tells himself: *"Maybe she's just running late and she's still in the bathroom or something."*

He calls the number back. It rings twice then cuts itself off. Eschewal grips the phone and sits down.

He can feel his rage rising inside him; he's pissed, more pissed because he got all spruced up with nowhere to go.

# Chapter Fifty-Six

**PEACHY SITS IN HER** bedroom alone, hoping Eschewal gets the message and does not call back. She decides to call Deuce to ask if they can link up. Deuce lies and tells her he will call her back in five minutes.

Ten minutes pass and Peachy is getting anxious, she's about to call Deuce back when a withheld number flashes up on her screen. Without thinking, she answers expecting to hear the voice of Deuce, instead she hears the voice of Eschewal.

The reality of what Peachy has been doing, avoiding his call, hits Eschewal between his chest plates and makes him weak.

Eschewal controls his rage and in a smooth tone, he questions: "So what, are we still linking up?"

Peachy clears her throat and feels her legs go weak as she gets ready to lie. "Oh I'm so sorry, babes, something has come up so I can't make it."

Eschewal grits his teeth as a lump appears in his throat. He replies: "So you couldn't call from before and let me know?"

Peachy slips out of the question. "Nah, cause I just

found out now, init."

Eschewal once again calms the rage from exploding on Peachy's BS and firmly says: "This thing that has come up, exactly what is it?"

"It's just something, init," Peachy hesitates then adds, "I just got to do something."

With the first trace of anger in his voice, Eschewal retorts: "That's what I want to know, what have you got to do?"

Peachy stays quiet as her mind goes blank from trying to make up a good enough reason.

"Oi, are you listening?"

Peachy remains quiet. This makes Eschewal's voice rise higher with anger; he can't control his emotion. "That's why I know you're an idiot, you can't even answer man."

Eschewal grips the phone. His body shaking with anger, he wants to curse Peachy out and say: *'Oi when I see you, I'm gonna lick you over and buss-up your face. Respect something, you flipping butters.'* But the thought quickly disappears as Eschewal knows that thug inside him died a long time ago.

He ends the call and throws his phone on the table then sits down. The anger hasn't fully left his body, when his phone begins to ring. He jumps up thinking it's Peachy, instead it's Deuce inviting him to a rave.

Eschewal takes a moment to decide. The repetitiveness of going out to raves and events just so he could see the girl in the park again has taken its toll on him. Before he had a purpose, now it just seems there is no need but reluctantly he agrees. After all, he's spruced up and at least now he has somewhere to go.

# Chapter Fifty-Seven

· **THE RAVE IS PACKED** with females, but as they walk past Eschewal, he takes no notice of them. He no longer has the energy to look; he spent a year looking for that girl in the park and nothing. Eschewal closes his eyes and not really thinking clearly, he says to himself: *"Maybe Deuce is right; I should stop looking and just bang different chicks until I find the one. I think it's time to let the dog run wild."*

Eschewal has given up hope of finding a wifey and becoming happy. He will let the dog take over from here. He opens his eyes so the dog can be set free to pounce.

Two females swoop past him. His eyes become gripped on the one behind. Eschewal mumbles: "Rah, she's pretty." A moment passes, suddenly his sub-conscious sends alarm bells to his memory. His legs go weak, he loses his breath, he can't believe it: *it's the girl in the park!*

Eschewal's feet seem stuck to the ground as his insides begin to shoot an array of emotions, leaving his arms dead and his fingers tingling. Eschewal's heart begins to flutter. He bites his lip and wishes he never had sex but had held out like he planned. It would have made this moment ever so perfect.

A smile spreads across Eschewal's face, as he realises not everything in life can be perfect, and for the first time he truly feels happy to be alive. He has finally found her and isn't going to lose her again.

Eschewal looks over at Deuce and says: "Oi, I'll be back in a minute," then steps down the stairs to meet his princess.

# Chapter Fifty-Eight

**ESCHEWAL ENTERS THE DOWN-STAIRS** bar area. He stops and begins to look around. His heart rate has fallen back to normal but is on its way back up. He thinks for a moment that he has lost the girl again. Then finally, his eyes fall upon her. She stands by the bar, her beauty glowing and captivating him.

Eschewal smiles. *'What a life'*, he thinks, *'just when I gave up hope and least expected it she steps back into my life.'*

Eschewal takes a deep breath, all his nerves have disappeared, he feels calm and confident. This is his lady he has nothing to be afraid of.

Eschewal borrows a pen from a sweet-boy, writes his number down, and begins his approach. He reaches the girl, grips her wrist and leans in, then says: "If you want to find out how a real man treats a woman, give me a call."

He smiles, she smiles, and his breath is taken away on seeing her beautiful teeth. Then smoothly Eschewal passes her his number, but before he leaves, he says: "Sorry, where's my manners. Would you like a drink?"

Once again, the girl reveals her beautiful teeth. She shakes her head and mouths: "No thank you."

Eschewal nods his head. "Okay, I'll wait for your call then."

Cool as possible, Eschewal walks back out of the girls' life, wondering whether he has done enough to become a part of her life. Only time will tell.

*"Yeah only time will tell,"* Eschewal says to himself while walking back up the stairs.

His last thoughts before reaching Deuce are: *'Was it a mistake not to ask for her name?' 'Nah,'* he thinks, *'if it's not meant to be, I only want to remember her as,* **THE GIRL IN THE PARK.**

# THREE DAYS LATER

# Chapter Fifty-Nine

**NIGHT HAS FALLEN. SALACIOUS** has company inside her low-ceilinged, wide-windowed flat. She walks from the kitchen back into the sitting room with drinks.

"So what, are you gonna tell me the secret you've been hiding for the past two months, or what?"

"Hold your horses, I'm about to tell you now, init. Eya." Salacious hands a drink over to her guest, she sits down, crosses her legs and begins: "Well, you remember when we talked about our fantasy."

"Yeah," replies her guest with excitement in her voice.

"Well…" Salacious bites her lip, "I did it."

"Did what?" asks her guest, because she remembers talking about three different fantasies.

"You know…" Salacious sticks two fingers in the air. "Two guys."

The guest screams: "You little tart!" She covers her mouth. "Oh my god! Tell me everything. How was it?"

"I don't remember much of it, but you remember how I'm always complaining that I've never been satisfied? Well that all changed." Salacious begins to giggle; you can't tell whether it's from nerves or embarrassment.

The guest puts her hand over her mouth again. "I can't believe you done it. How do you feel now?"

Salacious shrugs her shoulders. "I dunno, the same, but you know I don't feel dirty or nothing cause at the end of the day they didn't sex me, they sexed the condom."

Salacious takes a sip of her drink and is about to continue. The guest butts in with: "So who are these guys?"

Salacious shakes her head. "I don't know. I'm really bad." Salacious begins to laugh then continues: "The one who spoke to me first is called Ricky. He offered me a lift home and I said yes, and then gave him my number. He called me later on that night then I met him with his friend and went back to his friend's house." Salacious takes two sips of her drink then continues. "I wasn't even going to go, but that bastard began messing around again." 'The bastard' is Salacious' boyfriend. "Yeah, so I just said what the hell and went."

The guest laughs. "You're really bad." She puts down her drink and adds, with a hint of sadness: "I told Peen yesterday, we can never get back together."

Salacious stays quiet. She loves her friend to the extent that they tell everyone they're cousins, and for ages she has heard her friend say: *That's it, me and Peen are over.* Only to discover that a few days later they're back together and going through the same drama: him beating on her because she found out (again) that he had been cheating on her.

The guest picks up her drink. She knows what Salacious is thinking. "Nah listen," the guest takes a sip, "I'm serious this time. I even took this guys number at that rave I went to at the weekend, and I'm gonna call him now."

Salacious smiles. "Yeah, who is he? Where's he from?

"I don't know, he gave me one cheesy line but he was so sweet," replies the guest, as she takes out her phone and dials the number.

# Chapter Sixty

**ESCHEWAL IS IN HIS** sitting room talking with a close friend. They are discussing life, as a call comes through.

"Yeah, hello. Who's this?" says Eschewal. He pauses for a second then looks at his friend. He doesn't believe that he just heard what he heard. "Sorry, say that again."

"It's the girl that you gave your number to at the club on Saturday, don't you remember me?"

Again Eschewal pauses in silence. The first emotion to hit him makes him feel like stripping off his clothes and running down the road naked, screaming his excitement.

"Yeah, of course," answers Eschewal controlling his excitement. "So, anyway I didn't get your name."

With a hint of amusement and seduction the girl replies: "Oh, it's Manna."

Eschewal doesn't know it yet, but the name Manna will ring in his subconscious for many a year to come. "Okay is that like 'da manna?' Or does your name mean something else?"

A few seconds pass... Eschewal pulls the phone away from his ear then puts it back. "Yeah, hello-hello." The call has been disconnected. Eschewal feels like throwing the phone on the wall. He thinks that Manna might think he hung up the phone on her. He begins stressing that she won't call back and because she withheld her number he cannot call her back.

Eschewal sits there for a while staring at his phone. His friend asks: "What's up, bruv, everything cool?"

Eschewal swallows the lump in his throat. "Yeah, man."

"So who was that on the phone?" questions the friend.

Eschewal replies quietly: "Arh, no-one, man." As he ends his sentence his phone begins to ring. He looks at the display; a number which he does not recognize flashes up. Eschewal's heart screams out: *This must be her, his princess, this was meant to be!*

"Yeah, hello," Eschewal's voice shoots down the phone with haste.

"Yeah, it's me, sorry about that, babes, my battery died."

Eschewal lays back into his chair and replies coolly: "Nah, that's cool, babes. So what were you saying?"

And what Manna had to say led to a three hour conversation. By the end of it Eschewal had found out almost everything about her life and visa versa. The conversation ended with a date set for the weekend and that night when Eschewal went to bed, he did not sleep.

# THE WEEKEND

# Chapter Sixty-One

**ESCHEWAL IS STRESSING, HE** has a problem: his car is still in the garage and it won't be ready until tomorrow. He paces the sitting room holding his phone, wondering what to do. He knows this is the big test. Will Manna pull out of the date because there is no ride or will she prove to be the real woman of his dreams?

Eschewal takes a deep breath and calls Manna. "Yeah, hello. Is this Manna? Yeah, hello, yeah it's me, Eschewal... Yeah, what's up, babes? Oi listen, my car's in the garage." Eschewal is about to explain that he won't get the car back till tomorrow, when Manna butts in with: "Nah, that's cool, babes, I'll take a bus and come and meet you."

In that moment, Eschewal wants to bend down on one knee and propose marriage as he feels love strike at his heart.

"Eschewal, are you there?" questions Manna.

Eschewal feels like he is about to shed tears. He swallows hard then clears his throat. "Yeah, yeah, so you know how to get to the cinema then?"

Manna sweetly giggles, she can tell that Eschewal is shocked by her response. "Yeah, babes, I know where it is. I'll meet you outside there at eight."

"Okay, bye." Eschewal ends the call and just stares at the floor, he feels it is too good to be true; that a girl who looks as good as Manna isn't superficial. A smile begins to stretch across Eschewal's face as he enjoys the happiness which begins to run through his body. Eschewal snaps out of his trance and heads for the sweet-boy preparation.

# Chapter Sixty-Two

**THE BUS WHICH ESCHEWAL** is on shoots up the hill towards the cinema. He's sitting at the front of the double decker bus, looking out the window. His thoughts are running wild, he thinks: *'Why couldn't pay day be this week?'* he would have sent a cab to pick Manna up. Now he thinks he looks like a Joe pinch penny but what could he do? He is about to spend all the money he has and that money is his lunch money for the rest of the week. He will now have to eat buttered bread for the week and drink water from the free vending machine that his company provides.

Eschewal's palms begin to sweat. His insecurities kick in. He tells himself that maybe Manna won't turn up. *'She's too good for me.'* he tells himself, *'I don't deserve someone like her. People like me aren't allowed happiness. I don't deserve her.'*

Eschewal feels like getting off the bus and going home. Before he acts, words from the black book come to mind, it reminds him: *I am a producer of values and no longer a destroyer of values and that is where true self-esteem begins to grow from, but to keep it growing I must never go back to being a destroyer of values.*

Eschewal begins to feel good about himself, well he has done more good than bad and he will always keep on doing good.

The bus pulls up at the cinema. Eschewal feels his legs go dead and with his heart beating fast, he steps down the stairs. Eschewal bounces off the bus and sitting so patiently on the bus bench is Manna. Eschewal's heart melts as Manna's beauty feels like it is suffocating him. He plays it cool then remembers to breathe.

"Oh, I'm not late am I?" he asks with a cheeky grin.

Manna looks at her watch. "No, I'm early," she says with a great big smile, as she gets off the bench.

Eschewal leads her to the cinema entrance. As they step through the doors and to the ticket office, then buy popcorn, Eschewal hopes Manna hasn't noticed that he hasn't taken his eyes off her. Eschewal wants to fall into her wide seductive eyes, he doesn't know who is more fortunate him or her. He is going to love her like she never knew love before.

For the first time, as the film begins Eschewal reaches out and takes hold of a woman's hand in public. Eschewal feels electricity run through his body. He looks at Manna, he rubs her hand, they exchange smiles then turn their heads back towards the film.

# Chapter Sixty-Three

**THE NIGHT AIR IS** cool, even though it is the start of winter. The usual busy main-road has only a few cars shooting up and down it. Eschewal leads Manna towards the street crossing, they cross over to the other side of the road and begin walking in the direction of the bus stops.

Eschewal calculates how much money he has left; it is just enough to drop Manna home in a cab. The couple are approaching the strip of road where the bus stops, cab station and food outlets are. Eschewal contemplates what to do: escort Manna home in a cab then walk back home or simply invite her back to his yard and work from there.

The pair begin to speak at the same time. Eschewal ends his sentence, "...something to eat?"

"Yeah, I am a bit hungry."

Eschewal says to himself: *"Damn, why am I fronting. I don't have enough money to buy food."*

His chest begins to tighten up. The only option he has is his credit card, which is almost maxed out.

Eschewal finally replies: "Okay, let's get something

to eat. What do you feel for, pizza?"

"Yeah, I don't mind."

Eschewal and Manna head towards the pizza restaurant, but it has already closed. Once again, Eschewal's chest begins to tighten. He was looking forward to spending more time with Manna. He looks over at the takeaway. He can't really see Manna coming home with him on the first date to eat a takeaway. However, his heart says something different. "Would you like to get a takeaway and come back to mine?" asks Eschewal, almost holding his breath.

Manna smiles. "Yeah, why not?"

The tension runs out of Eschewal's body as his eyes widen and a huge smile appears. He leads Manna over to the takeaway, then in a cab onwards to his house.

# Chapter Sixty-Four

**THE LIGHTS ARE DOWN** low, Eschewal and Manna have plates of food on their laps. They sit and eat in comfortable silence with just smooth music humming in the background.

Eschewal can't remember takeaway food ever tasting this good. Manna has an effect on him because every spoonful he eats, it just tastes sweeter and sweeter.

The food is finished and the couple begin talking for the next two hours then, as casual as possible, Manna slips into Eschewal arms. Instantly, Eschewal grows an erection, but it's not an erection full of lust that would make him just want to start sexing, it is evenly balanced out with a deep resonating love. For the first time in so many years, Eschewal's heart is overflowing with happiness and he owes it all to Manna.

Eschewal smiles as he definitely now feels there is no longer the need to become a creator of values; he has all the happiness he needs.

He looks down at Manna and watches her fall asleep in his arms.

# Chapter Sixty-Five

**IT'S A CHILLY SUNNY** Monday morning and Manna sits at her desk with a grin on her face. She can't stop thinking about the other night that she spent with Eschewal. She is wondering why he had not tried to have sex with her. After all, she did end up in his bed with only her knickers on. It was the first time for her that she had allowed herself to be in that position with a man and he had not tried it on. All night long Eschewal had only held her in his arms, even though his penis was rock hard almost the whole night. This had made such an impression on Manna that she was slowly falling for him. This emotion puts a smile on her face. She feels like phoning Eschewal, just to hear his voice. In that same moment her phone begins to ring. She digs down into her purse. Her heart flutters as she wonders if it's Eschewal. The name on the phone flashes up Spiv.

Manna answers it filled with joy in her voice. "Hi yah, babes."

"Yeah, what you saying?" responds Spiv

"Nothing, I'm just at work, init."

"So, how you sound so happy?"

Manna pauses, she wonders if she should tell Spiv about Eschewal. *'Yeah, I might as well,'* she thinks. "Nah, it's nothing, it's just that I've met someone."

There is a sudden silence as jealousy runs down Spiv's spine. He thinks: *'After all the work I put in with her, now some fool is going to mess that up?'* He plays it cool, controls his vexation and makes Manna feel that he's happy for her. "Is it, don't lie?" he begins with fake excitement in his voice, "where did you meet him?"

"Um, last week Saturday at your club night," replies Manna.

Spiv begins to search his memory bank, on who was there. There were so many players. "Okay, so what's his name?"

"Eschewal... Why, do you know him?"

"Nah, nah," replies Spiv. He considers asking what Eschewal looks like, but decides not to. Spiv swiftly changes the subject.

The moment Spiv gets off the phone he begins his investigation on Eschewal. There is no way he's going to lose out on the time invested in being friends with Manna, just so he could get into her knickers.

# Chapter Sixty-Six

**THE CHILLY SUNNY MORNING** ended and brought with it a cold-fresh-crisp night and a full moon, shinning high in the sky. Deuce is on his way over to Eschewal's house, he has a new link for him and Eschewal. The link has dreams of her and Deuce being lovers, Deuce has other ideas.

Deuce pulls up two streets away from Eschewal's house and dials Eschewal's number. Eschewal answers.

Deuce begins his pitch: "Yes, blud, what you saying...? Hey, I've got a big link for me and you, blud. One sexy chick, she's on it."

Eschewal bluntly replies: "Nah, bro, I'm not on it." Deuce feels his legs go weak because he had slipped and was spotted kissing a girl as she stepped out of his car by his wifey's sister. That night when he went home his main argument was: *"Nah, babes the girl's my work mate and I didn't kiss her, she kissed me and it was only a friendly kiss on the cheek after I dropped her to the bus stop."*

His wifey wasn't convinced and Deuce knew he

couldn't risk having any girls in his car again. Desperation bubbles within Deuce because without Eschewal he can't meet his link tonight.

"So why are you not on it, blud?" questions Deuce as he bites down on his lip.

Eschewal swallows as butterflies sink to the bottom of his stomach. He retorts: "I've met my wifey, blud. I'm telling you she's the one.

Scornfully Deuce says: "How you mean, she's the one? Listen, you can't just trust any girl. I told you before every girl that I know are cheating bitches. I'm telling you, that's why I do what I do."

Eschewal almost sucks on his teeth as he says: "Bruv, I'm not watching that, if she wants to cheat on me, that's up to her, but I will never cheat on her, and that's real."

"So what you saying, you're not gonna come on this link?"

Eschewal shakes his head not caring that he has now revealed he is no longer a player and says: "Nah, I've told you, bruv. I've met my wifey, it's long."

Hate, spite, madness twist themselves in Deuce's throat, he can hardly get the words out. "Alright, blud, alright. I'll talk to you later."

Deuce grips his phone tightly. He feels like smashing it on the window screen. *"Cunt,"* says Deuce to himself, *"after all the links I brought him on, he was just trying to find a wifey? Liberties."*

Deuce leans back in his seat and stares out the window as he begins thinking of a way to get back at Eschewal.

# Chapter Sixty-Seven

**SPIV HAS JUST STEPPED** into his house. He has been trying all day to get through to Deuce. He finally gets a ringing tone.

Deuce's phone vibrates in his pocket. He lets it ring for a while then without removing his stare, he uses his earpiece and answers the call.

"Yeah, hello... who this...? Who?"

"Me, blud, man, Spiv. You going on like you don't know man's voice, what's wrong with you?"

Deuce coughs. "Nothing, man, I'm just chilling, what's going on?" Deuce wonders if he should invite Spiv on the link. He decides not to, because Spiv loves to show off his wealth around links to make Deuce look small.

Spiv lowers his voice before he speaks. "Oi, cuz you listening?"

"Yeah, go on," replies Deuce.

"Oi, do you know someone called, Eschewal?"

Deuce thinks for a moment, then says: "Nah, nah, why?"

Spiv sucks on his teeth. "Listen you know my ting,

Manna? You know she just told me that she linked some yute last week at my rave. You know I'm mad for dat."

Deuce doesn't care less; he has his own problems to deal with, but he fronts. "Yeah, rah that's nuts, boy."

"I know, bruv, I need to find out who this yute is, star. I can't make him take away this chick, I've been on her too long, you get me?"

"Yeah," replies Deuce, "I know how you feel, bruv but forget bout dat. You know rass-clart Eros try say he's found a wifey and linking's long. After all the blud-clart links I brought the yute on." Deuce wipes the corners of his mouth, then continues: "Imagine that, when we was skinning out that link, he wasn't chatting that shit. Dick-head, flipping dick-head."

Spiv's attention is brought back into the conversation, he has zoned out for a while. He didn't give a damn about Deuce's problem with Eschewal. What he wanted to know was why he didn't know about this threesome until now. "Which ting is this? What's her name?" questions Spiv.

"Some ting, init. Rah, what's her name again… Oh yeah, Salacious."

"Salacious," Spiv pauses, "um, where she come from?"

"From the ends, init."

"Yeah, what does she look like?"

Deuce sucks on his teeth. "Some pretty ting, fit, nice. Why?"

"Because you know who I think that is? That's rass-clart Manna's cousin, trust me that's Manna's cousin."

"Don't lie! Rah boy, me and Eros bun her boy, mash her down."

"Yeah, better that. Anyway I'm gonna go, I have to call around and find out who this yute is. So are you sure you don't know who he is?"

"What's his name again?" questions Deuce.

"Eschewal."

Deuce pauses for a moment, "Eschewal... um, what does he look like?"

"I don't even know," replies Spiv.

"Where's he from?"

"I don't know, cuz, he must be from the ends."

"Oi, hold on," begins Deuce as his memory about Eschewal's history comes back to him. "Isn't Eros's name a pet name?"

Spiv shakes his head. "Arh, I don't even know."

"Yeah, bruv, I remember now. Eros's real name is Eschewal." A sinister look crosses Deuce's face. "Yeah, you know, I totally forgot; true say everyone has always called him Eros. And trust me I'm sure he is the only Eschewal on the ends."

Spiv has lost his breath for a while, but now has it back. "Yeah and the little pussy hole was at the club last week, init? It must be him."

"It's him, bruv, he's taking the piss. Listen just ask Manna, yeah, if this yute is also called Eros. Then just break his legs and tell her about Salacious, no long ting."

Spiv's eyes light up. "It's true, alright, brother safe, I'm gonna give you a ring back, peace."

# Chapter Sixty-Eight

**SPIV CALLED MANNA STRAIGHT** after, but she has already turned off her non-personal phone.

It is an hour later. Manna and Eschewal are snuggled up on the sofa. The stylish chrome fireplace blows out warm heat, the lights are dimmed low and the TV is playing slow jam videos. Eschewal's penis is rock hard, it's beating against Manna's bottom, she can feel it and it's turning her on. Her nipples stiffen, Eschewal grips her tighter, but doesn't grind on her. He slips his fingers in-between Manna's and moves his body further onto her. He sniffs the scent of her hair and kisses her head gently, then sniffs her scent again. He feels love seeping through. Eschewal closes his eyes, a smile crosses his face. An image of him and Manna married with two children stains his imagination. He sees his future similar to the life which his grandparents had: a nice well-kept house, good food always cooking on the stove, a nice large family car and a garage. What gives Eschewal the most excitement is the idea of him working hard to support Manna and their new family.

Eschewal drifts off into a sleep with the feeling that,

for the first time in his life, his future is bright and nothing can go wrong.

*'The black book wasn't right, I didn't have to become a creator of values to receive happiness and riches.'* These are his last thoughts before he falls into a peaceful sleep with Manna in his arms.

# Chapter Sixty-Nine

**IT'S THE FOLLOWING DAY** and Manna kisses Eschewal on the lips, without tongue, and jumps out of the car, she almost skips to her front door. Manna turns and waves goodbye. Eschewal notices her smile, the type of smile that beams not only from the mouth but from the eyes. That would be the last time Eschewal would ever see it again, that great big smile.

Manna closes the front door, she rests her back onto it for a while and feels like screaming with joy. She gets herself together and blows out air, then makes her way to the bathroom. She pulls out her non-personal phone and turns it on. The phone beeps then flashes up a message. She listens to it before setting the bath. It's Spiv and he sounds urgent. Manna plans to call him back after taking a bath but before she can get undressed and stick the phone on the charger, the phone begins to ring.

"Hey, what's up girl?" asks Spiv.

"Hold on," says Manna as she sticks the charger on the phone. "Yeah, nothing much, I'm just about to step in the bath."

"Okay," responds Spiv, "did you get my message?"

"Yeah, what's up?" questions Manna as she sits down on her bed and unclips her bra.

"Nah, I just want to ask you something. I was talking with one of my friends, yeah... Listen you know that yute you was telling me about, is he also called Eros?"

Manna pauses for a second. "Um, why?"

"Ter, listen I found out something yesterday, that I think you should know."

"What?"

"I don't know if I should tell you the horror."

"Just tell me man, go on," pleads Manna.

"Well listen, if he's also called Eros then I heard he ran a battery on your cousin, Salacious."

Horror, distress and confusion explode within Manna. Her heart seems to sink down to her big toe. She doesn't want to believe it but deep down she thinks it might be true.

"Oi, Manna, are you there?"

Manna regains her voice. "Yeah, yeah, I've got to go, I'll talk to you later."

Manna has a plan. Her hand trembles as she pushes the send button, Eschewal's name flashes up on her screen.

# Chapter Seventy

**ESCHEWAL SPINS ON HIS** heels and slides across the floor as if he is performing and singing on stage. He is on his way to meet Manna and surprise her with a romantic night out. He puts the final touch to the sweet boy preparation and steps out the door.

It's only been two days since he has seen her but it feels like two weeks; he's even happier because Manna has invited him to her house. Unknowingly, it's a set up. Manna plans to display a picture of Salacious and when Eschewal arrives she'll inform him that the girl in the picture is her cousin and best friend. Manna will then wait to see if Eschewal admits to knowing Salacious and how.

Eschewal has arrived at Manna's house. His heart is racing as he waits for the front door to open. Manna opens it with a forced smile. Eschewal notices but thinks nothing of it, he bends over and gives her a kiss.

Eschewal follows Manna into the living area. With the most natural manner she can manage, Manna points at Salacious's picture, which is perched atop the TV.

"Arh, that's my cousin and best friend, Salacious," she says.

Slowly Eschewal moves towards the picture. As the face comes into view his legs begin to go weak. He can feel his heart snap at knowing the only girl that he could ever love at that moment has disappeared from his life. Eschewal regains his composure and looks over at Manna to see if she has read his facial expression.

Manna has her back turned, she doesn't want it to be confirmed that way. As Eschewal begins to speak, shivers run down Manna's spine.

"Oi, Manna…"

Manna wants to block her hearing.

"Um listen," begins Eschewal, "I've left my phone in the car. I'm just gonna go down and get it, yeah?"

Manna unfreezes, she relaxes, and then nods her head.

Eschewal walks out of the room and heads outside, he needs time to think.

# Chapter Seventy-One

**ESCHEWAL PUNCHES THE AIR**. He feels as if a heated knife is stuck in his heart. He shakes his head, knowing that he's lost her, the only woman he could ever love. Eschewal sighs. He was planning to start saving for the next five years and then buy Manna a beautiful ring, get down on one knee and propose marriage.

Eschewal closes his eyes and thinks back to the black book. He wonders if his loss of interest in becoming a creator of values, after he first saw Manna in the park, is the reason behind him losing Manna. He feels it might be. He thinks hard on what the black book would suggest he do in a situation like this. The only thing that comes to mind is: *fully integrated honesty.*

Eschewal grits his teeth and heads back up the stairs. He has decided to be fair with Manna and will not continue the relationship on deceit.

Eschewal enters the room, he looks into Manna's eyes. The thought crosses his mind to say nothing but he knows that would only cause his true love long-term pain. Eschewal could never do that, he loves her so much already.

It feels like a nightmare; it feels like it isn't him telling Manna how he knows the girl in the picture.

Once the last word jumps off Eschewals lips, the heartbreak that sweeps over Manna's features is visible.

# THREE WEEKS LATER

# Chapter Seventy-Two

**AFTER THE SADNESS SWOOPED** over Manna's face, every night Eschewal dreamed he would touch her face again. But Manna had chosen her friendship with Salacious over a possible happy and loving marriage. Eschewal had lost the love of his life but learnt a deadly lesson: most people don't want fairness. Manna would have been happy if Eschewal acted as if he had never seen Salacious before. She would have been glad to be kept ignorant.

Eschewal holds onto the bathroom sink, he looks into the mirror and sees a different face, it is not the face of three weeks ago. The happy face that Manna gave him, the face that finally had something to smile about. His insides are getting ready to cry but he won't let himself release tears.

Eschewal releases his grip and nods his head. It's time to let go and move on. A tear almost falls. He asks himself: *"How can I move on without Manna in my life?"*

From the moment, he saw her in the park it was love. Love that would never go away. It was true, it was real, and it was powerful. No matter what anybody says: *"That wasn't love, it was only lust because you can't love someone that quick. You don't even know her for long enough."*

Nope. Eschewal knew this was not true, because what he felt, he could not control. What he felt could only be love. What he felt had even made him forget about becoming a creator of values and receiving the happiness & riches the black book had promised.

Eschewal shakes his head. He now has to get used to living his life without the love of his life. The corner of his mouth turns down and he wishes he could have plucked up the courage and told Manna he had spent one year searching for her.

Eschewal huffs and leaves the bathroom wondering: *'Would she have even cared or would it have made a difference?'*

# Chapter Seventy-Three

ESCHEWAL ENTERS HIS SITTING room and plonks himself in front of the TV, as usual after his boring day at work.

It is a Friday evening and he is about to settle in for a night filled with reality shows and comedies when his phone rings. He jumps up with his heart pounding, wishing it's Manna. He sucks his teeth as Deuce's name flashes up on the screen.

Deuce hopes he has timed things perfectly. He reckons that by now Eschewal will have got Manna enough out of his system to become a player again.

Deuce received a call from Spiv moments after Eschewal had told Manna what he had done with her cousin. Spiv went on to being the shoulder for Manna to cry on and later he became the main man in Manna's life. Spiv finally had his prize, he had not yet decided what route to play on Manna; whether to sex her for a few months then dash her away or make her his baby mother then dash her away.

Eschewal answers the phone. "Yeah, mate, what's up?" he asks bluntly.

"Rah, you sound upset, bruv, what's going on?"

"Nah, man I'm safe," lies Eschewal. "I'm just tired, man."

"Yeah," Deuce pauses, he wants to laugh but controls himself and continues: "So what, you linking wifey tonight?"

Eschewal feels a lump rise in his throat. "Nah, nah, me and her done, bruv."

Deuce holds back another laugh. "What, already? What happen?"

Eschewal blows out hot air. "Ter, bruv, you're not gonna believe it, you know the girl invited me to her house and the moment I step in the door, she shows me a picture of her cousin. Ter, and guess who the cousin was? The same chick we mashed down in my yard."

Deuce quickly pulls the phone away from his ear and bites his lip so he won't crack up laughing. "What, don't lie, is it? So what happen?"

"I told her, init. I told her about the threesome."

Deuce's mouth drops. "What, are you nuts? You can't tell certain girls them things. You can't be honest with certain girls. Listen certain girls expect to be lied to, they love being treated bad it gives them something to complain about, init. Look at me and my wifey. I don't stop give her bun and she don't stop call me a bastard and a dog but she won't leave me, cause I won't admit nothing. Come on, bruv, that's the game, gee. Lie and cheat and don't get caught, then it's all good."

Eschewal shakes his head. "Nah, I'm a different yute, I can't live my life like that."

Deuce raises his eyebrows and taps his steering wheel. "Bruv, what's happened to you? You never used to be like this back in the day."

Eschewal thinks for a moment whether he should tell Deuce the reason why he's changed is because of the black book. Eschewal decides not to and lets Deuce continue.

"Come on, bruv," begins Deuce, "you should forget about that nice guy shit, because all the girls who I know, think that all guys are bastards and dogs." Deuce licks his lips. "Oi, anyway forget about her, she weren't meant for you. Listen, if you're on it I've got a link for tomorrow, you know?"

Eschewal pauses in thought... Linking back with Deuce is the last thing he wants. But he has come to the conclusion that the reason he lost Manna and lost his chance of happiness & riches was because he forgot about becoming a creator of values. He still feels that getting a wifey will make him become a creator of values and guarantee his happiness & riches. Therefore he is sure if he continues to find a new wifey and not forget about becoming a creator of values, happiness & riches will be his forever.

"Yeah alright, bruv I'm on it. I'll link you tomorrow." Eschewal ends the call and grips his phone, he smiles. He is ready to hit the road again but this time he will not forget about the ultimate goal.

# Chapter Seventy-Four

**WHEN ESCHEWAL PICKED DEUCE** up from his gates, the sun was still up in the sky. The winter sun is on its way down, turning day to dusk as Eschewal drives down a road filled with a hundred shops, selling everything from alcohol to gravestones.

Deuce turns down the volume of the music and grips his phone. "Little bitch, little rass bitches, little jezzys!" he says, then looks over at Eschewal. "I'm telling you, you know, bruv, these girls are fools you know, they're stupid, blud. You get me? It's a good-ting I've got this other link lined up."

Eschewal takes his eyes off the road. "So what, are these other links nice then?"

"Yeah, man," lies Deuce he purposely chose these links over the other ones because the other ones were too pretty. He just couldn't risk Eschewal falling in love with one of them because he now feels Eschewal will never become a player again but will keep him as his lift-boy until either Eschewal finds a wifey or his wifey gets wise of Eschewal's car.

"Yeah, their kinda nice still," Deuce flicks his nose

and switches back to talking about the pretty links who he is pretending blew him out.

"Yeah, but them other bitches, man," Deuce says, lying about the pretty links. "They've got me mad, try-lock off their phone on man. Little waste-chicks. I swear if I ever see them, I'll give them one box in their face. Yeah I lick that over, star. Make them know that I'm not a rass idiot, you get me doh, blud?"

Eschewal nods his head and keeps on driving. He's hoping he will be able to turn this link into his wifey.

# Chapter Seventy-Five

**THE TIME IS FIVE** minutes to twelve. Eschewal has his link sitting on his bed. He shakes his head then looks over at the girl. He begins to focus on the best parts of her. He looks at her hair, which is nicely kept. That is the best part of her, he thinks.

Eschewal places both legs on his bed and says: "Oi, how come you're sitting way over there, you're not scared of me are you?"

The girl shakes her head. "No."

"Well come here then."

The girl slides over and lies across Eschewal's lap. He begins stroking her hair. She looks up and smiles revealing short wide-spaced teeth. Eschewal feels this is the worst part of her but if looked at another way it makes her look cute. Eschewal decides to test the waters. He leans in for a kiss…. her mouth tastes fresh. He pulls her buttons and fights with her belt; finally he gets her jeans down.

Eschewal and the girl begin to fondle and kiss. Eschewal has his eyes closed and Manna pops into his mind. He now throws the girl over and deep French kisses her while bumping and grinding. "Mmm," says Eschewal. The girl grips him behind his neck and says: "Ohh baby, I want you."

Eschewal responds with kisses up and down the girl's neck then in a low whisper adds: "Arh, Manna I want you too."

The girl moves her neck away from Eschewal's mouth. "What? What did you call me?"

Eschewal opens his eyes and coughs. "Err? Um nothing, man."

"Oh," responds the girl then gives Eschewal back her neck.

Eschewal gives the girl a kiss on the forehead and says: "Nah you know what, let's chill for a minute."

"Why, what's wrong?"

"Nah nothing," lies Eschewal as he puts his arms behind his head and thinks: *'I can never fake liking someone. It has to be real.'*

"Hug me, please," says the girl.

With vexation on his face and guilt in his heart Eschewal turns around and hugs the girl while knowing he will never link her again and she will never know why.

Eschewal closes his eyes and drifts off into a dream, wishing he had Manna in his arms.

# Chapter Seventy-Six

**THE WEEKEND WIND DOWN** is taking its toll upon Eschewal on this Monday morning. He only went to bed four hours ago and is now sitting in front of his computer wishing his private spaceship would beam him up. Eschewal rubs the corners of his eyes and blinks twice. He feels his brain hurt; the tiredness is killing him, from trying to stay awake. He closes his eyes for a moment and contemplates: *'I might have to put some poisonous caffeine in my blood to keep me awake.'* As Eschewal opens his eyes, in steps who he thinks at first is Manna. Eschewal's heart skips a few beats, he is now fully awake.

The manager introduces the girl: "Hi everyone. This is Reasha, the new temp. She'll be with us for a few days at least, so please make her feel at home."

The manager directs Reasha over to her desk, which is two desks behind Eschewal's. It's like falling in love all over again. Reasha wears her hair the same way as Manna, thrown back away from her face revealing a beautiful smile with good teeth. Reasha is even about the same height as Manna, her shoulder dropping just beneath Eschewal's armpit.

Reasha smiles as she steps past. Eschewal sniffs and a sweet scent of peaches hits him, he nods his head and thinks: *'Yeah, lunch time I'm gonna make my move.'*

# Chapter Seventy-Seven

**LUNCHTIME ARRIVES. ESCHEWAL SPENDS** most of the morning wondering what approach to take with Reasha.

Eschewal watches as Reasha eats the last of her sandwich and rises from the table. His palms become sweaty, his heart rate speeds up, his legs go weak, his mind spins into the world of self-doubt.

*"What if she blows me out?"* he says to himself. Eschewal has decided on the smooth-sexy approach with a bit of ruff. *"What if this approach is wrong? Should I go for the respectful-modest approach? Damn, which one should I use?"* Eschewal breathes in and out heavily. *"Damn, be cool fool."*

Calm and steady, Eschewal stands up. He leaves his plate behind and paces Reasha towards the exit. Unaware, Reasha walks through the swinging doors to the lifts. Eschewal smoothly follows up behind.

As the lift door opens he grips Reasha by her arm. "Excuse me," he says looking deep into her eyes, "I know you're not gonna keep acting as if you ain't noticed me watching you?"

Reasha smiles. She replies: "Yeah, I've noticed, but why didn't you say something to me in the office?"

Eschewal releases his grip but keeps hold of her hand. He strokes it tenderly and says with a ghetto tone of voice: "You listening, it's true say I don't want people to know my business, you feel me?" He doesn't wait for a reply, quickly adding: "So what, can I get your number?"

Reasha smiles and nods her head. Eschewal takes out his phone and punches in the number.

# Chapter Seventy-Eight

**ESCHEWAL ROLLS OVER ONTO** his front and stretches for the phone. He looks at the time. It reads nine thirty pm. He thinks: *'Yeah, the perfect time to call a girl who might be into watching soap operas.'*

Eschewal sits up and dials the number… four rings later, it's answered.

"Yeah, hello," begins Eschewal, "is this um, Reasha?" Eschewal waits for the reply, then goes on. "Arh yeah, what's up, babes? This is Eschewal from work, you remember me, yeah?"

Reasha licks her lips and says in a sweet tone of voice: "Of course I do. I only met you today, I'm not that bad."

Eschewal laughs then says: "Okay girl, so what you up to anyway?"

"Oh I'm just chilling, watching some rubbish on the TV."

Eschewal smiles and with charm in his voice he says: "I'm glad I'm not disturbing you, because I wouldn't want to start off on a bad foot."

"No, you're doing just fine," replies Reasha with a

giggle.

Eschewal begins the get-to-know-you conversation. "So apart from watching TV what else do you like doing in your spare time?"

"Oh I like to read and listen to music."

Eschewal jumps on the music reference, which he plans to use as the lead up to the date suggestion. "Oh, so what type of music do you like then?"

"Um, you know I like a bit of everything."

"Yeah, me to. So what, do you go out raving a lot?"

Reasha turns over the TV onto a music channel then answers: "Nah, not really I mostly go to wine bars, if I go out."

"Hmm, you like going to wine bars? Yeah I prefer going to wine bars myself than raving."

A moment of silence passes. Eschewal quickly follows up with getting the answer to the most undesirable qualities that he dislikes in a woman. "So do you smoke and drink?"

"No, I don't smoke but I do drink. Only when I go out though."

Eschewal is happy enough that Reasha only drinks. He can work with that. So he decides to jump straight in with the date suggestion.

He invites her to a wine bar at the weekend, where they play live music by chic musical artists. Reasha accepts the invite with excitement.

Eschewal goes over the date details then ends the call.

# Chapter Seventy-Nine

**DEUCE SITS IN HIS** parked car, two streets away from where Eschewal lives. He has just received two links and needs help. Deuce activates Eschewal's number and waits for it to be answered. Eschewal hears his phone ringing but is in no hurry to answer it as he sees Deuce's name flashing on the screen.

Eschewal adds the finishing touches to his sweet-boy preparation and replaces the bottle of sweet scent back on the table. He rubs the liquid on the side of his face, around his neck and over his ears. His phone is still ringing. He picks it up and walks towards the front door and reluctantly he puts Deuce out of his wait. "Yes, blud. What's going on, bruv?"

With a pissed off sound in his voice, Deuce answers the question with a question. "How you took so long to answer the phone, blud?"

Eschewal sucks on his teeth. "Just cool, man, I'm just about to step out, init."

"Yeah, where you off to?" Deuce does not wait for Eschewal to answer. "Because you know I have a link for me and you. A big link this time, blud. Both of these chicks are heavy, criss, blud, trust me."

With a smile on his face, Eschewal replies: "Nah I'm going on a link now, blud."

A jealous rage fires up in Deuce at knowing that Eschewal got himself a link and didn't even think to bring him in on the friend. With much effort, Deuce holds down the rage from exploding and says: "Yeah, true stories, who's that then, cuz?"

"Some chick that I met at work, she looks alright still."

Deuce's lips turn down into a smirk as he says: "So what are you looking to chop it tonight, then?"

Eschewal walks up to his kitchen to double check that all fires and electrical points are turned off as he answers: "Boy I don't even know, blud, cause I feel say she might be a jezz but an undercover jezz. You know the type, to hold back the sex on the first night." Eschewal doesn't believe his last statement himself, he only said it to try to deter Deuce from asking to be brought in on a threesome, but without knowing, Eschewal has fallen into a trap.

"Yeah," begins Deuce with cunningness. "She seems long, bruv. You should blow her out and come on my link, cause it's definite sex we're sexing and trust me these tings are criss."

Eschewal swallows hard. He wishes he had courage to come out and say: *"Bruv, don't you know I'm not player no more. I don't want to sex different chicks. Laow me please and help me find a wifey."*

Instead he uses his diplomatic tone of voice and says: "Arh, blud, I can't blow her out, cuz, she's waiting on me now, and look how late you rung me with your link. Just cool, man, and put your link on pause for another time."

Deuce nods his head but not in agreement, he's getting his sex tonight before going home to wifey, someway, somehow.

He grits his teeth and hides his disappointment as he says: "Alright, blud, it's all good. I'll check you tomorrow yeah... yeah-yeah, peace."

Deuce grips his phone, leans back into the chair and contemplates.

# Chapter Eighty

**FIVE HOURS LATER THE** date has ended. Eschewal has Reasha wearing her sexiest dress which reveal her tiny waist. Eschewal is happy enough with the physical, and during the five hours that they have spent so far, he feels a connection with her mentally.

Eschewal pulls his car up to his gates and stops just behind Reasha's parked car. He is glad that she drove down to his house for two reasons. He now has the chance to invite her up and even if she says no, he does not have to drop her home.

Eschewal locks off the engine, the sound of music sucks itself back into the speakers. He looks over at Reasha, he can tell she doesn't want the night to end right now so with confidence he suggests: "So, do you wanna come up for a while?" Reasha pauses with her answer. Eschewal jokingly adds: "For a cup of coffee or something."

Reasha smiles. "Yeah I'll come up for a while and chill, why not?"

Eschewal's heart skips a beat as the dog jumps on his back and arouses his penis. He pops the car door and steps out, quickly he dips his hand into his pocket and pins his erection up into the left corner of his boxers. He closes his door and waits for Reasha to close hers then leads her to his front door.

# Chapter Eighty-One

"YEAH, LET ME TAKE your coat," says Eschewal as he pushes open his sitting room door and invites Reasha to enter.

Reasha's eyes swim around the trendy decorated living space, then she comments: "Arh, your place is nice. I like the way it's not crowded with too much furniture."

Eschewal removes his eyes from Reasha's juicy backside as it moves with a life of its own, and replies: "Oh, thank you." Eschewal coughs and pins up the coat. "So um, would you like a drink?

"Yes, thank you," replies Reasha.

Eschewal smiles. "Okay I'll be back in a minute," he points his finger, "You can take off your shoes you know, get comfy, man."

Reasha wrinkles her nose. "Nah, I'm okay."

Eschewal nods his head and leaves the room. Moments later he and Reasha are caught up in stimulating conversation, sipping on soft drink. The conversation ends and only the sound of the TV remains.

Eschewal turns his face to Reasha. His lips move but

not to release words, they connect on Reasha's beautiful lips. Eschewal's tongue shoots into Reasha's mouth, her tongue shoots back, in and out they go. Both now feeling friskier, they start to grind at each other. Eschewal stands up and bring Reasha up with him. Kissing and groping Eschewal leads Reasha to the bedroom. He throws her on the bed and climbs on top. He grinds for a moment or two then begins to pull off her shoes. She stops him and smiles. "Wait a second," she whispers. Reasha gets up and takes off her clothes and shoes, she puts her shoes by the doorway and steps back over to Eschewal in her underwear.

Eschewal grips her by the waist and pulls her to the bed while spinning over on top of her. He slides his body between her open legs then grips them and pushes them in the air. Her feet brush past his nose; the smell of cheesy feet turns his stomach.

Reasha pulls Eschewal's hand towards the front of her knickers. He pulls it away and kisses her on the lips, then sits up. "Listen, babes," he begins, "I think we're moving too fast. I like you nuff so I wanna take it slow, you get me?"

Reasha does not reply; she feels confused. It's usually her saying those words. Eschewal kisses her again. "I'll be back in a minute," he says and walks off to the bathroom.

# THE FOLLOWING
# WEEKEND

# Chapter Eighty-Two

**TWO PHONES BEGIN RINGING** at the same time. Deuce picks up one of them, looks at the name flashing on the screen and rejects the call. Without looking at the screen on the other phone he answers the call. He knows who is calling from the ring tone.

"Yeah, what's up, babes?" Deuce doesn't give his wifey a chance to answer as he dives in with: "I was trying to call you back, but I couldn't get through, what's wrong with your phone?"

Deuce's wifey quickly calms herself from exploding. "What do you mean what's wrong with my phone? Nothing's wrong with my phone. When we talked earlier and we got cut off, why couldn't I get back through to you?"

Deuce begins to explain: "Yeah, babes, I was up in that wine bar chilling with my work mates when you rung, babes."

Deuce's wifey remains quiet and just wishes she had proof that Deuce wasn't in the wine bar.

Deuce continues: "I must've lost the reception init, so I went outside and got back the reception, then tried to call you back and couldn't get through, babes."

Deuce waits for his wifey to respond. While he waits, his thoughts travel to what really happened.

*After drinking a quick drink with his work colleagues, he left with a female one, offering to drop her home. The colleague had once given him oral sex in the stationery cupboard at the last Christmas party.*

*Without warning Deuce parked his car on a dark street, hoping to get a quickie. While caressing the girl, he threw down some sweet talk, but the girl was not having it because she was on her period. Deuce felt like hitting the steering wheel when she told him. He really wanted to get some sex tonight. Instead he pulled out his penis and the Christmas party came flooding back.*

*Five minutes in and before Deuce could get that tingle in his leg that leads to it shaking then him discharging in the girl's mouth his phone began ringing. He recognised the ring and shouted out: "Shit!" The girl pulled away her mouth. Deuce pleaded for her not to stop as he reached for his phone and rejected the call from his wifey. He held the back of the girl's head and pulled it towards his penis while saying: "Come on, finish it."*

*The girl pulled away and said: "Nah, I think we better stop."*

*Deuce sucked on his teeth and didn't argue. He started the car and drove the girl home.*

Deuce's thoughts are broken by the sound of his wifey's reply. "Yeah, whatever Deuce. There's nothing wrong with my phone." She sucks on her teeth. "So anyway, when am I gonna see you?"

Deuce deepens his voice. "I told you tonight, init?

I'm just gonna take care of something and then come around. Stop stressing, man."

The wifey cuts her eye. "Alright, Deuce. I'll see you later, bye."

Deuce sits back in the chair, looks up at Eschewal's window, and sucks his teeth. He puts his car into reverse and parks three roads away then makes his way back to Eschewal's house.

# Chapter Eighty-Three

**USUALLY ESCHEWAL WOULD HAVE** been more careful at moving the curtain to see who was knocking at his door. But due to his mind penetrated by thoughts of his second date with Reasha he cracks the curtain a bit too much. He would have had time to crack it back if only Deuce had taken his eyes away for a spilt second.

Deuce looks over at Eschewal, his eyes glint with a hunger for raw animal sex. The five-minute taster he received earlier has wet his appetite, the only problem is he does not have a link.

"So, bruv you mean to say you're going out with this chick again and couldn't link me with the friend?" asks Deuce with a slight hint of anger in his voice.

Deuce's tool of guilt makes Eschewal feel bad but he shakes it off and decides to be honest.

"Ay, cuz. I'm gonna be real, blud, you see this ting here, I'm looking at her to be my wifey and you dun know if I link you with one of her friends you're just gonna hit it and run." Eschewal slaps on some of his sweet scent. "Yeah, you get me, then that's gonna be long term problems for me, cause my ting now is gonna be digging me out asking why I linked her friend with a dog."

Deuce sucks on his teeth and abruptly replies: "Oi, blud stop chatting shit, man. Don't watch dat. Man's big people, blud. You can't control what I'm gonna do." Deuce gets up from the seat so he can express his point. "Yeah, alright then so what? I link the friend, I sex her but it don't work out, that's not your fault."

Eschewal shakes his head. "Yeah, I know that, bro but you're not listening. I don't want the headache and let's be real here. You're not linking her with the intentions of hoping the link will lead to something, because you dun got your wifey already, so be real."

Deuce's nostrils flare. He wants to lash out at Eschewal and call him bad-mind. "Alright, that's real. I ain't got intentions for the link to go anywhere, but forget 'bout dat because you know you ain't linked me with nothing, blud." Deuce digs his fingers towards the floor. "Since we've been moving you ain't given me nothing, you get me?" With desperation in his eyes Deuce demands: "Give me something, blud, give me something." Deuce wipes the corners of his mouth. He had to get sex tonight to be able to handle the horror of the verbal abuse from his wifey.

Eschewal looks at the time; he's gonna be late and needs Deuce out of his house, so he hands over Keneisha's phone number. "Eya call this ting up," Eschewal decides to add a bit of hype. He lies: "Yeah, bruv, this thing has a fat pussy, trust me it's buff, you're gonna enjoy it."

Deuce's eyes widen as he begins punching the number into his phone. "What, are you sure? Don't try give me no idiot ting you know."

Eschewal doesn't reply. Deuce presses send.

# Chapter Eighty-Four

**KENEISHA IS LYING IN** her knickers and bra with her eyes fixed to her wall-mounted TV as the call comes through. She lets the phone ring, while deciding whether to answer a withheld number.

Keneisha is feeling depressed and doesn't really want to talk to anyone, especially someone she may not even know. The shotter, Godfrey who Keneisha blew out Eschewal for, had told her when they first met that he had a wifey and he wasn't going to leave her. Keneisha had hoped that she could convince him otherwise. After more than a year she's given up.

The phone stops ringing then seconds later it begins ringing again. Keneisha answers: "Yeah, hello," she says while rolling into the S position. Her face shows puzzlement. "Who?"

Deuce repeats: "It's Mark. I must've met you like a couple months back and you gave me your number."

Keneisha smiles and wonders if it's Godfrey playing games. Keneisha acts the fool and plays along. "So where did you meet me then?"

Deuce keeps his cool and replies: "I'm sure I met

you at a rave somewhere but I can't remember what rave."

Keneisha laughs. "But I hardly ever rave. The last rave I went to was about a year ago, so I don't know where you would have seen me to get my number." Keneisha waits for Deuce's reply: she doesn't get one. "So you say your name is Mark? Are you sure your name is Mark? Do you happen to know a Godfrey?"

"Nah, babes. I don't know a Godfrey." Deuce decides to just put it on Keneisha.

"Look, at the end of the day I got your number and it's no biggie to come link me, and if you don't like what you see then you can blow. So what you saying?"

Keneisha smiles, she feels like going on a mini adventure, to relieve some of her depression.

"Okay, MARK! Text me your number, then I'll text you where to meet me."

Deuce licks his lips. "Alright cool," then ends the call.

# Chapter Eighty-Five

**DEUCE LOOKS OVER AT** Eschewal with a smile. "Yes, blud, she's gonna text me where to meet her. What is this ting a jezz?"

Eschewal lies, he shrugs his shoulders and answers: "I don't know, blud, all I know is she loves sex but loving sex is different from having sex with many men on the same day."

"What, she loves sex? Does she suck hood and that, yeah?"

Eschewal nods his head and lies again. "Yeah course, that's standard." Eschewal begins circling his head up and down. "And she can suck it good too." Eschewal adds more hype. "Oh shit, she can suck a hood, bruv. She'll make your eyes pop out your head, star."

Deuce becomes light-headed. He gets butterflies and his body begins to overheat. His eyes widen, a grin spreads across his face revealing a mouth full of teeth. Deuce lives for the build-up before the link. Eschewal knows this and knows Deuce will now leave his house happy and content with the link.

Deuce claps his hands. "Alright, bruv I'm gonna blow, I'm gonna link up this ting." Deuce extends his fist and hits it on Eschewal's, while saying: "You're still fuckrie doh. Don't get it twisted, but it's all good, you see me?"

Eschewal responds with a smile and a jerk of the head, then says: "Just make sure you wrap it up before you slap it up."

"Alright, gee, little more from now." Deuce leaves.

Eschewal slaps on some more sweet scent then hits the streets for his second date with Reasha.

# Chapter Eighty-Six

**THE DATE HAS GONE** well. Eschewal took Reasha to a comedy night where they laughed and sipped on drinks. All that laughing had taken away Eschewal's worries.

His worries have now returned. Eschewal looks down towards the side of Reasha's face. He smells her hair; it's smelling good. The clean scent from her clothes catches his nostrils. Eschewal closes his eyes and wants to say a prayer, asking for Reasha's feet not to be smelling. He wants to pray that even if they do still smell he will be able to overlook it and fall in love with her.

Eschewal opens his eyes. Reasha turns her face towards him and notices his intense look.

"Is everything alright, babes?"

Eschewal clears his throat. "Yeah, man, everything's criss, why?"

Reasha leans off her elbows. "Nah, you just look like you're not really here. I mean, like your thoughts are distant. As if you're staring into space. What's on your mind?" Reasha unlocks herself from Eschewal's embrace and sits up so she can take a better look at his eyes.

"Nah, nothing's on my mind," lies Eschewal smoothly as he looks away from Reasha's stare. How can he tell her that he has been stressing all week to find out if her feet still smell?

"Nah, sometimes I just zone out and meditate, you get me?"

Reasha nods her head but feels for some reason that there is more to it than just meditating.

"I understand. I'm gonna call you my spaceman."

Eschewal laughs. Reasha gets up from the chair. "I'm just going to the bathroom, I'll be back in a minute."

Eschewal swallows hard as he watches Reasha leave the room.

# Chapter Eighty-Seven

**REASHA CLOSES THE BATHROOM** door and moves over to the toilet. She picks up the seat, pulls down her garments and sits down. Reasha doesn't really know what is gwaning with Eschewal but she feels maybe it could be to do with the smell of her shoes. *'But I placed them almost out of the room, he could never have smelt them. It must be something else,'* thinks Reasha. She bites down on her lip and wonders: *'So why didn't he go thru, what game is he playing, does he have a girl?'* Reasha just doesn't know.

She closes her eyes and thinks about the game she'll be playing tonight, it's called the tight jeans game. This is where she will firstly make Eschewal fight to take off her belt. Every time he gets it undone she will buckle it back up. After maybe fifteen minutes of this she will leave it unbuckled then make Eschewal begin to fight with her tight jeans. This is sure to leave him breathless, cause no matter how hard he tries those jeans won't be coming down unless he rips them off or Reasha stands up and takes them off. But Reasha plans to rise off the bed just enough to let the jeans be pulled past her hips then look Eschewal in the eyes and say: *"STOP, I think I'm coming on my period."*

Reasha smiles and stands up from the toilet. *'Yeah, that will send him crazy,'* she thinks as she pulls up her garments, takes off her shoes and leaves the bathroom.

# SIX WEEKS LATER

# Chapter Eighty-Eight

**AFTER REASHA LEFT, ESCHEWAL** slouched in his chair with his guts feeling twisted from disappointment. The disappointment then changed into guilt, as Eschewal remembers Reasha saying: *"Call me yeah,"* and him replying: *"Yeah, man, definitely."* Eschewal had swallowed the lie while thinking: *'Shit I drove another nail in the coffin that brands all men as bastards. If only I had the courage to let her know the deal.'* Eschewal shakes his head and slouches further down in his chair.

During the last six weeks, Eschewal has dated three different girls with three different problems that stood in the way of a possible relationship. Eschewal nods his head and thinks: *'It won't work out with any other girl because Manna is meant for me. She's the one who'll make me become a creator of values. I've got to get her back.'*

Eschewal jumps up and turns his house upside down to find Salacious's number. He eventually finds it and as he dials the number, his heart is beating, a hundred times a minute.

"Yeah hello, who's this?" demands Salacious.

Eschewal gathers his thoughts, he stutters: "It's

me."

"Who's me?" demands Salacious again.

"Me, man. Eros, don't you remember me?"

There is a moment of silence... "Yeah, what do you want?" replies Salacious with attitude.

Eschewal swallows his rage, as his old ghetto mentality hits him: *'Don't make no one take liberties, star.'*

"Hold on, do you have to talk to me in that tone?"

"Um well no, but you haven't ever called me before and now just out of the blue you're calling."

"Yeah I know, but you must know why I haven't called before."

Salacious lightly sucks her teeth. "Yeah, I know all about that, so why are you calling me?"

Eschewal swallows hard and thinks: *'Should I just pour my heart out and tell Salacious that I want her cousin so much that I searched for her for one year? That during that year, my only dream was to find Manna, marry her and love her forever?'* Eschewal ponders some more. *'Will she even care or even believe me? Will it make a difference?'*

Eschewal blows air through his nose, then answers: "Listen, I need to get Manna back into my life. I need you to give me her new number."

There is another moment of silence... "What, are you serious? Are you dizzy? Are you stupid? She don't want to know you. After what you told her. And how can you tell her something that was personal about me, huh?"

Eschewal does not bother answering. He hangs up the phone and just sits there, feeling broken.

# THREE WEEKS LATER

# Chapter Eighty-Nine

**ESCHEWAL'S HEART BROKE WHEN** Salacious spoke those words. He knew it was true, but wished it wasn't, so he could again see that great big smile that donned Manna's face the time he met her at the bus stop.

The traffic up ahead begins moving. Eschewal puts his brand new car into gear. He squints his eyes, then turns up the grimy beat. Rhythmically, he bops his head and a feeling of going back to his brief bad boy days filters through him. Back in the days he directed his ghetto mentality into channels of destruction and by doing so, boys feared him and girls loved him. He had respect, but at a price: the price of destruction to his soul and quality of life.

Eschewal shakes his head. In the beginning, he was glad the black book helped him redirect his ghetto mentality into positive channels. But right about now he is feeling those positive channels lead nowhere, except to the pain which he is feeling right now.

Eschewal moves off but is shortly stopped by another set of traffic lights. The feeling of just letting the dog rip loose and give up finding a wifey imbues him. Eschewal's jaw drops, his eyes become slits, he speaks to himself: *"I can't go on, bruv. It's all long, I'm gonna go back to being a player."*

He looks to his left then looks again, his heart races and his palms begin to sweat. He blinks twice as he watches Manna board a bus. The set of traffic lights let him go. He drives through them slowly letting the bus, which Manna has boarded, take off.

The thought of going back to being a player leaves Eschewal as he begins to follow the bus. He has a grin on his face and worry in his eyes as he wonders how Manna will react when he tells her what's on his mind.

Five stops up the road, Manna steps off the bus. She crosses over the road and waits at another bus stop.

Eschewal finds a nearby side road and parks his car. He quickly heads back over to Manna, forgetting that he came out to buy some clothes to relieve his depression.

# Chapter Ninety

**HOT FLUSHES SHOOT THROUGH** Eschewal as he approaches the bus stop.

He breathes in and out heavily as he calls Manna's name.

Manna turns her head. Her beautiful eyes connect with Eschewal. For a second he loses his breath…

"Hi, how you doing, can we talk?"

Manna almost sucks on her teeth. "Talk about what?" she says abruptly.

Eschewal is taken aback by her rebuttal but he composes himself.

"Talk about me and you," he says firmly.

"There's nothing to talk about, just leave me alone," replies Manna, as she looks away from Eschewal.

Eschewal pauses in thought as he contemplates whether to open his heart and soul and tell Manna how he had searched for her for a year and without her, life doesn't seem worth living. Eschewal nods his head and decides to tell her, not caring who hears.

Eschewal begins: "Nah, listen there is something…" but is cut off by a chunky looking guy who is sitting two seats away from Manna.

"Why don't you leave her alone, mate? She don't wanna know."

For a second, Eschewal can't believe his ears, he says: "What?!"

The chunky guy turns up his lips. "You heard the first time, mate. Leave her alone."

"Ter," says Eschewal as he feels that bad boy urge rise in him. He narrows his eyes and glares at the chunky guy. Eschewal bites his lip, his eyes turn stone cold. "Who the rass you think you talking to?"

The chunky guy replies: "You, init. What?!" and reaches into his bag to take out a weapon. Eschewal clocks this but doesn't care because the rage now running through him will numb any form of pain. This person has no idea that right about now Eschewal has the strength of ten men and would rip his head off.

Eschewal steps forward, and shouts: "WHAT?! Do you think you're greasy? You're not greasy!" Thinking: *'How dare this yute get involved with me and my happiness?'*

Manna jumps up. "Nah, don't fight, stop, stop!"

Eschewal looks into her eyes... his rage disappears. He backs off and sucks on his teeth. He reaches out for Manna's arm. "Can I talk to you, please?"

Manna pulls her arm away. "No, I can't, please, leave me..."

A bus pulls up. Manna runs to the open doors, Eschewal watches as she boards, followed by the chunky guy.

The idea of boarding the bus comes and goes.

Eschewal is about to cry as he watches the bus take Manna, once again, out of his life. He holds back the tears, replacing them with a feeling of hate as he wonders: *'Would Manna even care if I had the chance to break down and cry and tell her I searched for her for a year?'* *'Nah,'* thinks Eschewal as he walks back to his car. *'She wouldn't have cared, nobody cares.'*

# Chapter Ninety-One

AS ESCHEWAL DRIVES FROM his defeat, the sorrow inside him begins to pop and explode. It's almost unbearable. He can now understand why some people commit suicide. Eschewal has feelings to do something terrible to himself, or someone; to release the pain. Eschewal hits the steering wheel, wishing he had got on the bus and ripped off that person's face.

Eschewal begins fighting back the tears, he hasn't cried in years — since the time in hospital. Before that he had forgotten how to cry. The harsh streets, which grew him, would not stand for it. There were implicit rules not to show emotion, those rules were for street survival.

Eschewal quickly chokes back the tears and begins to man-up. *"It's nothing,"* he says to himself. *"Fire bun this. I'm just gonna go back to being a player. Fire bun Manna."*

Eschewal turns his car around and heads back towards a wide-hipped, fat-calf girl. He catches her just before she turns the corner. He beeps to get her attention. She stops and Eschewal jumps out of the car with his chest pushed towards the sky.

The girl responds well, she has a pretty face and her body is banging. Eschewal tells the girl he will call her later, then jumps back into his ride and drives off. As he drives, he begins to fight off a deep-seated feeling that maybe he should hold on and still pursue Manna. Eschewal shakes his head. *"Nah,"* he saw the hate in her eyes, it wasn't meant to be.

There goes that feeling again. It has Eschewal wondering: *'But was it meant to be? Her and me, me and her, Manna and me?'*

# LATER ON THAT EVENING

# Chapter Ninety-Two

**ESCHEWAL IS STEPPING THROUGH** his door with three shopping bags. He had spent five hundred notes on clothes just after getting that fat-calf girl's number. He throws the bags on his bed, then walks into his sitting room and sits in silence. The dog jumps on his back. Eschewal wants sex and wants it now. He takes out his phone and dials the fat-calf girl's number.

"Yeah, hello is this Kaya?"

"Yeah who's this?"

Eschewal clears his throat. "It's the guy who you gave your number to, about two hours ago."

"Oh, you alright? What are you saying?" replies Kaya.

"You tell me, init, what's going on?"

Kaya twiddles her hair and sits down on the bus stop bench, her fantasy floats her away for a minute. She already imagined marrying Eschewal and having his kids then living happily ever after.

"Arh nuffing much, I'm just going home." replies Kaya finally.

"Okay, so where's home?"

"Um, I live in south, init."

"Rah south yeah, that's my ends. So what you saying, what do you like doing?"

Kaya crosses her legs. "Um, I like going to the cinema, out for a drink, raving."

"Yeah," begins Eschewal as he rubs his chin. "So what, are you an adventurous person?"

Kaya looks confused. "Yeah, sort of but it depends on what you mean."

Butterflies hit Eschewal's stomach, he knows the next sentence could make or break the conversation. He goes for it. "I don't know, sexually. Like, do you enjoy sex?"

For a moment there is a slight pause. "Of course I enjoy sex. What type of question is that?"

Eschewal smiles. "Okay," he begins, "what type of sex do you like? Like, what's your best position?"

Kaya smiles and becomes flushed; it's a good thing that no one else is sitting at the bus stop. With her nipples pricking up, she answers: "Doggie style, I love doggie style."

"Geez, that's my best position too. So what else do you like doing? I bet you're a freak?"

"Yeah sometimes I can be, but I don't give head if that's what you're asking?"

Eschewal leans back in his chair. "What, you don't give head, are you serious?"

"Yeah, I have never given head before. I've had it given to me, doh."

Eschewal knows this is a hint to him; he plays it

cool. "So what you saying, you would never give head?"

Kaya swallows hard. "Yeah, maybe on the right person. So what, do you go down? Be honest."

"Yeah, but only if I had wifey."

This puts a smile on Kaya's face. Eschewal continues: "So what other freaky things have you done? Have you done anal sex?"

Kaya smiles. She has always wanted to try. "Nah, but I wouldn't say I won't because during sex sometimes it gets heated and anything could happen."

Eschewal raises his eyebrows. "True stories? So what, do you like riding it then?"

"Course."

"Yeah, but can you ride it good? Can you handle it?"

"Of course," replies Kaya.

"So what, have you ever been picked up while riding it?"

Kaya swallows hard again as she sees herself being picked up in strong arms and riding it.

"Nah never, no one has ever done that."

"For real? Well I'm gonna see what I can do about that. Trust me, I wish I could come and meet you now."

"So why don't you?"

Eschewal sits up, his heart begins racing. The dog is barking. "For real, where are you?"

Kaya shakes her head. "Nah, forget it... I've never done this before."

Eschewal calms his composure. "Do what before?"

Kaya bites her lip, she's feeling over-horny. "You know getting down on the first night."

"Nah, babes it's not that type of party, nothing can't go on unless you want it to go on."

Kaya thinks for a moment, she was only going to go home and be bored, so she decides to meet with Eschewal.

"Alright then, let's meet, but I'm serious. No funny business."

# Chapter Ninety-Three

**ESCHEWAL DASHES TO HIS** car. His phone begins to ring. He thinks it might be Kaya calling him with a change of mind. His heart shoots to his throat as Reasha's name flashes up on the screen. He hasn't heard from her for about two months and assumed she had got the message. Eschewal shakes his head, wondering what reason he could give her why he has not called since they linked last.

Eschewal clicks open his car door and answers the call: "Yeah, hello," he says with an even tone.

"Hi stranger," replies Reasha, as if it was just the other day they spoke. "What's up? Why haven't I heard from you?"

Eschewal swallows hard and ponders: *'Dare I tell her that because her feet smelt, I never want to link her on a sexual or romantic level again?'*

Eschewal clears his throat. "Nah, wait there, I'm sure you said you were going to give me a call and like, I've been waiting ever since."

Reasha wrinkles up her nose. "I don't remember saying that and even if I did say that, couldn't you call and find out why I hadn't called?"

Eschewal opens his car door then says: "Boy, to tell you the truth because you didn't call I thought you was giving me a sign that you wasn't interested."

Reasha raises her eyebrows and says: "Of course I'm interested in you." Reasha pauses then continues: "Are you interested in me?"

Eschewal closes his eyes and swings his car door open then shuts it. Time to be honest — Eschewal leans on the car roof.

"Yeah, man you're a nice girl, man."

Reasha clears her throat. "Yeah, but?"

"Nah, no buts. You're a nice girl, init." Eschewal opens his car door. "But listen, can we talk about this later, 'cause I'm in a rush to get somewhere."

Reasha almost sucks her teeth. "Yeah, okay."

"Alright, I'll call you later."

Eschewal ends the call with no intention of ever calling Reasha back, hoping this time she gets the message.

He jumps in the car and sucks his teeth then shakes his head. He thinks: *'Why couldn't I just be honest?'* but feels most people don't want honesty.

Eschewal sticks the key into the ignition and hurriedly speeds off, hoping that Kaya has not become fed up from waiting and left the bus stop.

# Chapter Ninety-Four

**OUTSIDE IS STILL LIGHT.** Eschewal storms his way to the bus stop where Kaya should still be waiting for him. He is weaving his way through the slow traffic in a now heated haste.

From out of nowhere, BANG! Eschewal hits into a station wagon. "SHIT!" shouts Eschewal. He bangs the steering wheel, he can't believe he's banged his brand new car bought just last week.

He pulls the car over to the side of the road while thinking: *'This must be a sign. I can't make the dog win. I have to continue and find myself a wifey.'* Eschewal gets out and looks towards the sky while he waits for the owner of the station wagon to get out of his car.

"SHIT!" Eschewal says again as he spots Deuce bopping out of a sweetie shop. Eschewal grits his teeth and wishes he could have hidden but it's too late, Deuce spots him and bops over.

Deuce waits, while Eschewal deals with the station wagon driver, but wonders if Eschewal has made it work with Reasha.

"Yes, blud," Deuce hits fists with Eschewal as the

station wagon driver walks back to his un-dented car.

Eschewal nods his head. "Yeah, wah gwan?"

Deuce shrugs his shoulders. "Boy, nuffing, I ain't seen you for long doh, bruv." Deuce had purposely stopped linking Eschewal because his wifey had got wind of Eschewal's car. But now that Deuce sees Eschewal has a new ride, Eschewal can become his lift-boy again. Deuce taps Eschewal's car. "So what, you got a new whip then, yeah?"

Eschewal smiles and nods. "Yeah," he says. Deuce returns the smile, "So where was you off to anyway?"

Eschewal lies: "Boy nowhere, man I was just cruis-ing init and that dick-head banged into me, init." "Yeah," Deuce sucks air through his teeth then with a joyful tone he says: "So what, give me a chick then."

Eschewal steps back, rubs his chin and jumps into the player role. "Boy I ain't got no links, blud. I ain't got nothing, cuz."

"So what happen to dat ting, last time?"

Memories of Reasha's smelly feet hits Eschewal. "Nah she was long, blud, you get me?" Eschewal sucks on his teeth. "I'm looking for something now, bruv."

With excitement in his voice, Deuce suggests: "Come then, let's go out there now and see if we can pick up some strays."

Eschewal feels like kicking himself. The last thing he wants is to start moving with Deuce again, but weari-ly he drives off with Deuce to one of the high street cor-ners.

# PART THREE

# THREE MONTHS LATER

# Chapter Ninety-Five

**LIKE DÉJA VU, ESCHEWAL SITS** with Deuce in his car on a corner. Eschewal looks at his phone. He's expecting a call from a girl who he chirpsed last week. She had promised that she would confirm the date a day ago. Eschewal sucks his teeth and puts his phone back into his pocket and thinks she wasn't the one. The real girl of his dreams who will make him become a creator of values might walk past the car at any moment. Eschewal puts the girl out of his mind and joins Deuce who's looking out for loose females.

"Rah, shit," says Deuce, "look at them two fit tings, blud."

"Where? Where?" replies Eschewal as he spins around, his head like a chicken.

"Over there, blud." Deuce points across the main road, the girl's are walking over the traffic lights.

Eschewal taps Deuce's shoulder. "Come, let's jump out and go after them."

Deuce shakes his head. "Nah, it's long." He wipes the corners of his mouth. "Bruv, you know I'm tired of chirpsing girls, tired of linking, bruv. But I can't stop. I don't know what's wrong with me, it's like if I don't sex a different girl at least once a week I can't function. That can't be right?"

Deuce pauses and looks out the window. "Oi, bruv you know how much girl I've chopped; young tings, old foots, all sorts." Deuce shakes his head. "I need to stop and marry my wifey, man."

Slowly Eschewal says: "Bruv, your problem is this: you have an addiction and like all addictions, you have to make a choice. Is there something in your life bigger than sex that would make you stop sexing different girls?"

Deuce thinks for a moment. There is nothing. Not even the love of his wifey.

Eschewal pops his door. "Oi, bruv, come. There's them same two chicks."

Deuce doesn't move as he thinks he will never be able to give up the game. He pops the door and joins Eschewal and the two sexy body girls.

# Chapter Ninety-Six

**THE SUN HAS FALLEN.** Deuce suggests a stroll in the park. After a half an hour drive, Eschewal pulls up at the park. Everybody steps out the car without coats because the day's blazing sun has left the night air warm.

Deuce, Eschewal and the two sexy body girls are sat on the freshly cut grass. They have been sitting there for almost an hour talking.

Deuce stares up at the stars. He says to himself: *"Flipping hell, once again little more from now I will be banging another chick that I just met and whose name I can't even remember. I need help."*

Deuce looks over at Eschewal, gives him the signal. Deuce coughs and stands up. "Eh, bruv I'm gonna see if I can get some drinks. I'll be back in a minute." Deuce looks towards his girl. "Oi, babes, you wanna follow me?"

The girl smiles and rises from the grass. "Okay."

The girl follows up behind Deuce, leaving Eschewal and his girl on the grass.

Eschewal leans back onto his elbows. The dog in

him raises its head; it wants him to talk the girl into having sex with him right now. Eschewal coughs and fights down the dog's temptation. He refocuses on getting to know this girl and maybe making her his wifey. "So," he begins, "you don't have a boyfriend right?"

The girl puts her hand over her mouth then removes it. "Yeah sort of, but we kind of broke up."

Eschewal's eyes soften. "Yeah, how long were you together?"

"Since school days."

Eschewal nods his head. "What, do you still love him?"

"Yeah," replies the girl softly.

"Wow that's deep. You know what? You should work it out, man. True love can come more than once but once you get it you should hold on to it and never let go."

The girl nods her head in agreement and leans back onto her elbows.

As she and Eschewal engage in further conversation Eschewal's visual picture, of him and her possibly living with happiness & riches, shatters into a thousand pieces putting him back to square one.

# Chapter Ninety-Seven

**OVER ON THE OTHER** side of the park, Deuce is sitting in a square courtyard with his girl. He dips his hand into his pocket and pulls out a condom.

"What's that? Is that a sweetie?" queries the girl.

Deuce smiles. "Nah, it's not a sweetie but it can make you feel sweet if you let me use it."

"Well if you tell me what it is I might?"

Deuce looks into the girl's eyes and smoothly says: "A condom."

The girl does not respond. Deuce adds: "So what, are you going to make me use it?"

The girl wrinkles up her nose. "What on me?"

"Yeah, obviously I'm not going to use it on myself."

The girl cracks a smile and shrugs her shoulders. "I dunno. If you want to."

Deuce's heart races. The dog is loose, he wants to fight it but it's no use.

The girl puts her hand on her hips. "What, are we gonna do it right here?"

"Nah, here's too bright. Let's find somewhere else." Deuce and the girl raise from the courtyard bench.

The wind begins to blow, while Deuce bends the girl over a park bench down by a darkened stream and begins sexual intercourse.

# ANOTHER THREE MONTHS

# Chapter Ninety-Eight

**ESCHEWAL STILL HAS NOT** copped a wifey or had any sex for over a year. Every girl he has linked has flopped, so this has now made Eschewal definitely think: *'These flops must be happening because Manna was definitely the one.'* Eschewal bites down on his teeth, as the thought hits him again: *'She had to be the one that would make me become the creator of values, because when I was with her I felt I could conquer the world.'*

Eschewal shakes his head and wonders: *'Could I become the creator of values without the love of my life? If so, what would be the use without the love of my life to share the happiness & riches with?'*

Eschewal sucks his teeth and twists in his chair. He looks at his blank computer screen. He bites his lip and remembers the moment he saw Salacious's picture. The feeling of being alive and happy began to drain from his body and just like that, Manna was gone.

Eschewal blinks his eyes and swallows hard. He quickly rises from his chair with a smile. He has been waiting for this wretched hour to come for the past four days so he can shut down his mind from work for a whole 60 hours.

Without saying bye to his colleagues, Eschewal almost runs out of his office and hits the warm fresh air. The headache he had before begins to evaporate as he disappears from his place of work.

# Chapter Ninety-Nine

**STARS ARE IN THE** sky and Eschewal finally reaches home after spending half an hour in traffic. He isn't going to let that get him down as he sits to eat the takeaway he has just purchased. He leans over to his phone and calls Deuce, who has another link for him. Eschewal's usual optimism that maybe this link is the one isn't as bold as it used to be. Eschewal secretly hopes Deuce will tell him the links have flopped.

"Yes, bruv. What, are those links still lined up for later?"

Deuce walks out of his bedroom leaving his wifey on his bed. He talks low: "Yeah, they're lined up, man. Just link me in about an hour. I have to get rid of wifey."

Eschewal bites down on his teeth and fills his mind with positive thoughts. *'Bruv, you never know, this might be the one,'* he muses then jokily replies: "Alright, my yute."

Deuce locks off his phone. Earlier he had lined up, what he thinks are two different sets of links, who are willing to bring a friend for Eschewal. But he now has to decide which link to blow out.

He walks back into his room thinking: *'I wonder which link to blow out? But they're both nice, man. But I think I should blow out Venisha, cause I've done hit her already. Yeah I'm gonna blow out Venisha and link Alena, plus Alena has got a cock-off bum.'*

Deuce jumps on his bed not realising he has an erection. His wifey notices.

"I hope that's for me?"

It isn't. Deuce is thinking about grabbing hold of Alena's big bum. He smiles, shivers shoot down his spine.

"Of course it's for you, babes. Come here."

Deuce spins his wifey back-ways and gives her sexual intercourse for ten minutes, feeling this will be enough to keep her sweet and send her on her way.

# Chapter One Hundred

**DEUCE HAS JUST BLOWN** out Venisha. She sits back down, vexed. She had gone and done her nails and hair for the double date with her friend, Deuce and Eschewal. Venisha sucks on her teeth, picks up her phone and dials her friend to let her know her link has flopped.

The phone answers. "Hi, babes."

"What's up sweetie?" replies the friend.

"Nothing much, just calling to say my link has flopped."

The friend replies: "Not to worry, babes. I've got back-up. Some guy just called me. I met him last weekend, he wants to link me and a friend."

"Really?" replies Venisha.

"Yeah," replies the friend. "So should I call him back and tell him yes?"

Venisha pauses. "Yeah, go on then, um what's his name anyway? Where did you meet him?"

"Oh his name's Mark. I met him while standing at a bus stop. He pulled up in a black sports car and you know I don't usually talk to guys who do that. But he got out of his car and came up to me."

Venisha's guts sink. Mark is the name she knows Deuce by and he drives a black sports car.

"MARK?" says Venisha

"Yeah, why, do you know him?"

"What does he look like?"

"Well, he's a pretty boy, tonk he's kinda choong still."

Venisha has her mouth open. "Oh my god, I swear down, he's the same guy who we was meant to link today."

The friend covers her mouth, then says: "Don't lie, your lying."

"I'm not, Alena. What's his number?"

"Hold on," says Alena as she flicks through her other phone. She reads out the number, it matches. "Bastard," curses Alena. "You see, that's why I hate players you know."

Venisha coughs. She feels a bit embarrassed that Deuce blew her out for Alena. Deep down, Alena feels chuffed that Deuce chose her but in the end, girls have to stick together.

# Chapter One Hundred and One

**DEUCE IS FEELING OVER-EXCITED**. He has got rid of wifey and the thought of sexing something new comes to mind. He can already see himself rolling Alena over and making her holler. A wide grin comes to his face as he finishes creaming his body down.

"Yeah," Deuce says as he pats his chest and moves over to his bottled sweet scents. As he begins to spray, a weird feeling comes over him. He stops in motion and wonders: *'Did I blow out Venisha too soon?'* Deuce thinks he must be getting soft in his old age because back in the day he was ten times as ruthless as he is now.

Deuce wouldn't ramp to make a link think that he's still coming and have the link waiting in the pouring rain. Deuce didn't care if the link spent half her day preparing. That didn't bother him, at the end of the day he always thought, there are more links where that one came from.

Deuce had been one cold-hearted ruthless player. He had shown no respect to females and got away with it, but now he was about to taste some of his own medicine.

Deuce's phone begins to ring. "Yeah, hello," he says with confidence.

Alena licks her lips then speaks.

# Chapter One Hundred and Two

**"OH, HI BABES," BEGINS** Alena as she looks over at Venisha and rolls her eyes. "Um you know what? I'm not going to be where I told you to pick me up."

Deuce's heart rate slows down, he relaxes. "Yeah, so where do you want me to pick you up?"

"Um," Alena bites down on her lip. "You know where I told you to meet me, yeah... well I want you to meet me outside the bus station on the main road instead, yeah? Someone's going to drop me and my friend off, so be there about half-ten."

Deuce wants to suck on his teeth because the arrangement was to meet at half-past nine, now he has to kill an hour. He really hated waiting around once he was ready.

Deuce looks up at the time, it reads seven forty-five, "Yeah alright," he finally says, "but I thought we said half nine?"

"Yeah I know," Alena pulls the phone away from her ear and holds back a laugh, "but I have to sort out something before I come, init."

"Alright, just make sure you're there you know,

don't let me have to wait around for you."

"Nah, I'll be there, babes, don't worry." Alena covers her mouth from laughing.

"Alright. Oi, Oi, Oi is the friend you bringing nice?"

"Yeah, man she's nice. Just like me."

Deuce nods his head. "Alright, later."

"Yeah, later," responds Alena as she ends the call and bursts out laughing.

Deuce throws down his phone onto his bed and continues getting ready with a feeling of uneasiness.

# Chapter One Hundred and Three

**ESCHEWAL IS TAPPING HIS** steering wheel as he and Deuce sit outside the bus station.

"Oi, where's these chicks, bruv, man?"

Deuce looks at his phone; the time reads 11:00 p.m. He feels like hitting the dashboard. He blows out air then leans back into the seat and grips the phone. "I don't know, man, they're taking the piss."

Eschewal squints. "Wait, are you sure this is the right place they said to meet them?"

"Yeah, man," replies Deuce as he screws his face and looks out the window.

Eschewal leans back his head. "Well I beg you call them then, cause it don't make sense we sit here like a pair of sitting ducks."

Deuce sucks his teeth and looks out the window. For a few minutes, there is silence between the men.

Eschewal gazes out his window and his thoughts drift to the time he saw Manna walk past him in the club. He feels the way it happened it seemed like magic brought her to him, to finally give him happiness, to give him something to live for. Eschewal feels like crying as he remembers how happy Manna made him feel for those brief moments he spent with her. Those moments felt like heaven, far from the hell which he grew up in and had to endure. Eschewal's chest begins to tighten, his eyes become slits, he still can't believe the way he lost Manna. Eschewal feels like hitting the steering wheel. He closes his eyes and thinks: *'I should never have forgotten about becoming a creator of values when I began looking for Manna because I'm sure if I hadn't, I would now have Manna in my arms and would be now living a life of happiness & riches.'* He shakes his head. Eschewal begins to feel that happiness is never meant for him. Eschewal opens his eyes. *'Nah,'* he thinks, *'I won't make it win. I didn't come this far to lose, I am not turning back. I'll find another princess and become a creator of values, no matter how long it takes.'*

Eschewal looks over at Deuce. "What, bruv aren't you gonna call them?"

Deuce sucks on his teeth. "Alright, man," then he dials Alena.

# Chapter One Hundred and Four

**ALENA JUMPS TO HER** phone. She sees Deuce's number and starts laughing. She had forgotten about Deuce, as her and Venisha get ready to go to a wine bar. She grips the phone and looks over at Venisha. "It's that fool. What do you think I should tell him now?"

Venisha shrugs her shoulders. Alena grits her teeth. The phone stops ringing. For a moment, Alena feels relieved until seconds later the phone begins ringing again.

Alena's eyes widen as she is hit with an idea of what to tell Deuce. She answers the phone. "Hi, babes, sorry about that, I was on my house phone." Alena bites her lip and paces the floor.

"Yeah," says Deuce, "so what's going on?"

"Agh, you know what," begins Alena while taking a breath, "the person who was meant to drop me to you, can't do it again."

Deuce curls his top lip. "So what, you weren't gonna call me and tell me this?"

Alena begins to say something, Deuce talks over her. "Yeah, man, I've been waiting out here like a fool."

"I'm sorry, babes, it's not my fault and plus I was trying to get another ride, that's why I haven't called you yet."

"Yeah," Deuce scratches the side of his mouth, "so what, did you get one?"

Alena looks over at Venisha and sticks out her tongue. "No, I couldn't get one."

Deuce almost huffs and puffs. "So what are you gonna do, then?"

"I don't know, like, why don't you come to my house."

Deuce flicks his nose. "Alright, so where do you live?"

Alena widens her mouth and eyes as she begins to give directions to Deuce. "Well you see the road that you're on, yeah, well drive down it and once you have passed the fourth traffic lights turn right and drive all the way down that road, yeah. Turn left then the second right and then you will see a tall block of flats called Shoot House, I live at number 18."

Deuce begins to smile, "Alright, I'll be there in a hot minute."

# Chapter One Hundred and Five

**ESCHEWAL SPINS THE CAR** off from the curb and heads for the fourth traffic lights.

Deuce points. "Yeah take this turning on the right."

Eschewal takes the turning and says: "Yeah, what's the next turning?"

Deuce leans back. "Um, I think it's the next left then the second right and we should see her block of flats."

Eschewal looks over at Deuce then back at the road. "Are you sure, bruv?"

"Yeah, man, what's wrong with you? Just drive, man."

Eschewal takes the left. Moments later he takes the second right in third gear and begins travelling down a long road.

"So where's her yard, blud?"

"Just cool, man. You haven't even got down half of the road yet."

"Yeah, but I can't see no block of flats up ahead. Are you sure this is where she said?"

Deuce sucks on his teeth and makes no reply. Eschewal has now nearly reached the end of the road without a block of flats in sight. He stops the car.

"This is long, man. Look, blud there's no block of flats. We must be on the wrong road."

Deuce sucks his teeth. Eschewal swallows hard. "Hey, bruv I beg you, call her again."

Deuce sighs then calls Alena, her phone is engaged and he feels like throwing his phone through the window. He sucks his teeth and says: "The phone's engaged."

Eschewal spins his car back around and drives back on himself. He spots a couple walking on the other side of the road. He swerves his car over to them and rolls down his windows.

"Excuse me," he says in his most non-threatening voice, "can you tell me where I can find..." Eschewal looks at Deuce, "Oi what's the name of the flats?"

"Shoot House."

Eschewal looks back at the couple, "Yeah, um, Shoot House?"

The couple think for a moment. "Yeah, um," says the female, "if you go back the way you came, once you get to the end of the road, turn right then take the third turning on your left and you can't miss it."

Eschewal nods his head. "Thank you." He spins his car around and hits 40 until he gets to the end of the road. Smoothly he takes the right. Steadily he drives up towards the third left feeling a bit pissed off that Deuce couldn't even remember simple directions. He takes the corner, a tall block of flats come into view. Eschewal smiles as he pushes his car up towards them.

# Chapter One Hundred and Six

ESCHEWAL PARKS THE CAR.

"What, call the chick then and let her know we're downstairs."

Deuce shakes his head. "I just called her, man, her phone is still engaged."

Eschewal nods towards the grey block of flats. "Well knock her up then."

"You do it, man."

Eschewal fires back: "I don't know her."

"Ter' so what, you're going on like you're afraid of girl. Just tell her you're my friend, init, and we're downstairs."

Eschewal sucks his teeth. "So what's her name and her flat number?"

Deuce wipes the corners of his eyes. "Alena, flat 18."

Eschewal steps out of the car. He reaches Shoot House and punches in 18. The intercom starts ringing, a man with a deep gravel voice answers. Eschewal pauses for a second and wonders if he has punched in the wrong number. He looks at the intercom, it reads 18 in large red numbers.

"Um, yeah, is um, Alena there, please?"

"What? Who?" bellows the voice in an exotic accent.

Eschewal repeats: "Alena, is Alena there, please?"

"Who, Alena?" Before the voice can continue Eschewal jumps in with: "Yeah, arh-leen-na," emphasizing the pronunciation.

"No, no. No Lena here."

"No, Arh-leen-na," shouts back Eschewal.

The voice shouts back with annoyance; he was in the middle of watching a porno and he wants to get back to it: "I said no Lena here!"

The man slams the intercom down. Eschewal feels rage run through him. He calms and tells himself maybe Deuce had misheard the girl so he calls bells, 28, 38 and 48. All come up fruitless. Eschewal walks away from the intercom, cursing under his breath.

# Chapter One Hundred and Seven

**ESCHEWAL BUSSES THE CAR** door and jumps in.

"What's up, bruv?" enquires Deuce.

Eschewal feels like laughing but the vexation doesn't leave his face.

"Dat weren't her yard, bruv."

"Are you, sure?"

Eschewal nods his head and blows out hot air. "Of course I'm sure, man. Some off-key man answered the door, man." Eschewal sucks his teeth.

"Ter," Deuce shakes his head, and then dials Alena. Her phone is switched off. "Bitch, flipping waste-chick. Try switch off her phone." Deuce looks over at Eschewal. "You see, bruv, what I'm saying about certain girls? They're bitches. You can't trust these hoes, man. They're probably linking next man, you get me?"

Eschewal makes no reply, all he can think about is the mistake he made in giving up on looking for Manna. He thinks: *'If I hadn't given up I would have never done the threesome on Salacious and would now be in the arms of Manna. Instead, I'm being poked in the arm by*

*Deuce.'*

"Oi, bruv, you get me?" Eschewal nods his head, Deuce looks away and stares out the window.

"Yeah, man. That's why man has to have a wifey. You get me? For times like this when bitches play games and you ain't got no other pussy to call. You can always go home to wifey."

Eschewal feels his insides twist, sending a sharp pain to his chest. The hope of finding a wifey and becoming a creator of values is over. The dog, which had almost laid silently asleep waiting for this moment to come, bolts to attention.

Eschewal slowly nods his head without realising he's about to have a mental breakdown.

Deuce scrolls to his wifey's name and sends a dialing tone. He says to Eschewal: "Yeah, gee take me home to my wifey."

With emotions balancing on razor thin wire Eschewal sticks the key into the ignition and drives off, knowing he will do something sick tonight.

# Chapter One Hundred and Eight

**THAT SICKNESS FINDS ESCHEWAL** standing in a phone box, the type of phone box, which is sign posted with sex for sale.

Eschewal shakes his head and says: *"Where did it go wrong? All I ever wanted was one woman. I dreamt of one romantic love, then becoming a creator of values and for once in my life experience real happiness."*

Eschewal feels sick, twisted and bitter. He has lost control and will now plunge into the dark depths of the world's corrupted soul.

Eschewal scans the various types of multicolored cards. His eyes fall on a picture of a young woman who claims she is new to the country and looking for a good time with a well-mannered gentleman. Eschewal studies her further: nice wide hips, round breasts and a pretty face. Eschewal begins to imagine sexing her, he sees the vision so he dials her number. It's engaged. Eschewal waits a while and calls back — It's still engaged — he calls back again — still no luck.

The dog is loose and out of control. Eschewal eagerly scans the other cards. His eyes drop onto the one pushed up into the corner. Eschewal removes the card and unfolds it. The picture of this woman is better than the one he was going to call. The only difference is it has the words, **BEAUTIFUL T-GIRL** in bold.

Eschewal is unaware what this means, he reads further.

*Pre-op t-girl (34C-24-34) extremely sexy, with full sensual lips, smooth long legs with a beautiful ass.*

Still unaware what the term t-girl means, Eschewal's palms begin to sweat as he dials for the t-girl... The t-girl answers.

# Chapter One Hundred and Nine

**TO ESCHEWAL IT FEELS** like he is moving in slow motion as he steps up to the intercom bell. He pulls his hat further down his face and takes a quick look either side of him and presses the bell.

A voice answers: "Hello," in a sexy tone.

"Yeah, hello, I just spoke to you on the phone."

Errrrhh, the door is buzzed open. Eschewal walks through it with his heart pumping. Just before he can make his way up, a head pops around the corner from atop of the stairs.

"Hello darling, are you here for flat 14?"

"Yeah, yeah," says Eschewal, as he climbs the stairs. He reaches the door, the t-girl seems stunned to see a person like Eschewal visiting.

"You here to see me?" asks the t-girl, while looking behind Eschewal to see if he has planned to come and do a robbery.

"Yeah, aren't you going to let me in?"

Slowly the t-girl opens the door. Eyes still showing worry the t-girl moves back.

Eschewal almost closes his eyes as he steps into the

hallway. As he moves down it, his eyes scan the carpet-decorated walls. He passes weird expensive looking paintings. Just before he reaches the bedroom, he picks up his image in the gold-plated wall mirror and for a split second the image he sees of himself he doesn't recognise.

# Chapter One Hundred and Ten

**THE T-GIRL CLOSES THE** door behind Eschewal and walks over to the bed. The scent of perfume on dirty skin hits Eschewal as he follows the t-girl. The smell slightly turns his stomach.

The t-girl wines sexily on the bed and asks: "So what do you want to do?"

Eschewal shrug's his shoulders. The t-girl's legs open. Seductively the t-girl rubs the groin area. "Like do you want, massage, sex?"

"Sex!"

"What type of sex you want, passive?"

Eschewal pauses. "What's passive?"

The t-girl's legs crosses. "Me, sex you."

"What?! Nahnahnah, me sex you." Eschewal's penis stiffens.

The t-girl's lips curl up. "How much money you got?"

Eschewal lies: "Eighty, that's all I've got."

"No, that's not enough." The t-girl stands up, "I told you one-fifty."

Eschewal fingers the notes. "Arh come on, all I've

got is eighty."

The t-girl thinks for a moment. "You got big cock? Let me see." Then reaches out to touch Eschewal's crotch.

Eschewal moves. "Just cool, man. What, you wanna see my hood? It's not that big." Eschewal pulls out his penis.

The t-girl's eyes widen. "Ohh, big cock!" The t-girl stands up. "Let's see if it's bigger than mine." The t-girl whips out a huge penis.

Eschewal's eyes almost pop out of their sockets. Now he knows what t-girl means: *a chick with a dick.*

Eschewal feels his body become light. A deep sickening sensation runs through him and like a shot, he bolts out of the flat.

# Chapter One Hundred and Eleven

**THE NIGHT-TIME AIR WHIZZES** past. As Eschewal runs and his lungs burn, he feels the first effect of his mental breakdown.

When he finally makes it home, he sits on his bed staring at the floor clenching his fist. The rage which seeps through him, instead of making him feel like he wants to explode, puts his mind into focus. He gets up from his bed, turns on the light and pulls out a suitcase from under his bed. He opens it and carefully removes the black book from the bottom of the case. Eschewal stares at the title.

**HOW TO CREATE YOUR DESTINY AND FOR-EVER LIVE LIFE WITH HAPPINESS & RICHES** Eschewal repeats the title to himself. He then opens the book and begins to read. He stops on the page that explains the role of consciousness. It says:

*Consciousness is the tool to create new values. The purpose for creating new values (that provide positive stimulation) is so that further values will flourish. Those who are aware of how to create new values that provide stimulation are those who run the world. Every need or want is con-*

*nected to the same essence, which is stimulation. Whether that is smoking on poison or promiscuous sex, it's the need or want for stimulation that drives us all.*

Eschewal turns the page and reads this paragraph twice. *Once disconnected from those destructive forces, you will unleash the power of your consciousness. This will give you the ability to become a creator of values. Then automatically happiness & riches will flow to you.*

He places his hand over the page of the book. His eyes show a hint of enlightenment, he feels he knows why he has not become the creator of values.

Eschewal thinks and says to himself: *"It now makes sense. I had to unleash the full power of my consciousness, to become a fully conscious being. Fully conscious beings who take action create their destinies and receive true happiness & riches."*

Eschewal smiles. He knows to become a creator of values isn't automatic on finding a wifey or disconnecting from the destructive forces.

He shakes his head as a deeper understanding hits him. *'I had to disconnect from the destructive forces first, to free my mind to think, then take action and jump from producing values (working a nine to five, etc) to creating values for others. Then happiness, riches and romantic love will follow.'*

Eschewal smiles once more at realising he does not have to find romantic love to become a creator of values. "I was putting the cart before the horse. All I've got to do is take action," says Eschewal silently.

Eschewal looks around his bedroom and thinks: *'What value can I create?'* He grips the book. An idea comes to him. He takes out his phone and scrolls down to Tek. The same guy he swore he would never phone again. Eschewal presses call... Tek answers.

"Yes, cuz what's going on, Tek?"

"Who's this?" says Tek sounding confused.

"It's me man Eros, what's popping?"

"Arh, Eros. I haven't heard from you for long. What's going on, gee?"

Eschewal's heart begins pounding as he tries to control his nerves. "Boy, nothing much, bruv. Oi you listening? Have you got any moves running?"

Tek raises his eyebrows. "Moves? But I thought you left the road ting long ago?"

"Yeah I have but you know how it is, life is hard. I got ber bills."

Tek smirks. "Boy I ain't really got anything running still I only got a little fraud ting running and... Nah forget about that you wouldn't be interested in that?"

"What, what is it?" eagerly questions Eschewal.

"Boy, it's the import ting init."

Eschewal nods his head and thinks: '*Yeah, that sounds like one of Tek's dodgy moves. Perfect, I'm bound to get caught and when I do I'll be locked away from my self destruction and be able to turn myself into a creator of values.*'

Eschewal's eyes light up as he sees his destiny — him as a value creator. He nods his head and says: "Yeah, gee I'm down with that."

Tek ends the call and puts things into action.

# EIGHTEEN DAYS LATER

# Chapter One Hundred and Twelve

**ESCHEWAL'S EYES SPRING OPEN** as the turbulence shakes the plane. He is on his way back from a sunny little island.

The content of his suitcase puts him back to focusing on his mission ahead. If it goes down right, Eschewal's emotional plan will hopefully wash away his "sins" and make him become a creator of values.

Eschewal looks out of the small plane window and stares at the clouds and thinks: *'But can I really do this?'*

Eschewal closes his eyes. A quote from a famous poet floods his mind. He recites the quote: *"Whatever you can do, or dream you can, begin it. Boldness has genius, power, and magic in it. Begin it now!"*

Eschewal opens his eyes and nods his head. *"I can do it. I'm gonna make my dream come true."*

Eschewal closes back his eyes as the plane ascends over his homeland. One heavy bump and the airport comes into view, Eschewal grips the arm rest. He looks cool and calm for what is about to go down.

Another bump and a jolt, the plane descends further.

Eschewal breathes easy as the plane touches the ground and rolls along the runway.

# Chapter One Hundred and Thirteen

**WITH STEADY STEPS, ESCHEWAL** walks to the baggage collection. He is carrying a medium-sized brown bag strapped over his back, which is filled with everything he will need for his trip.

Eschewal reaches the hallway of the baggage collection. It is filled with people waiting and dragging off their suitcases onto their trolleys. Eschewal looks up at the monitor hanging from the ceiling, which tells him which carousel has his luggage. Eschewal slowly walks over to carousel two, with his heart beating just a bit too much. He doesn't know it, but eyes behind walls are watching his every movement.

Eschewal reaches the carousel, he stands relaxed, saying to himself: *"It's gonna be all good, bruv. It's all good."*

Forty-five minutes later Eschewal still stands at carousel two. He spots his suitcase. His heart rate falls and a smile appears. He looks around the now half-empty hall and spots a few customs officers hovering about, Eschewal knows they're there for him.

With cool ease, Eschewal drags the suitcase from the

carousel and plonks it on the trolley. He looks left then right, then makes his way to the airport exit.

# Chapter One Hundred and Fourteen

**ESCHEWAL CAN'T SEE, BUT** behind him there is a swarm of customs officers running up towards him. They have been waiting for the word from the offices inside the baggage hall collection, that the suitcase has been picked up.

Eschewal is three feet away from where people are randomly called for a search. He looks at the officers; they are not looking in his direction. Eschewal feels for the first time that one of Tek's moves is going to work and he'll successfully smuggle 27 kilos of cannabis, until from behind, two different hands grip his arms. A voice says: "Excuse me sir, is that your suitcase?"

Eschewal blows out air and smiles. He nods his head and feels the officer's grip tighten on his arm.

"We have reason to believe that you have in your possession an illegal controlled drug. Please come with us."

As Eschewal is lead towards the airport holding cells, his thoughts run on what the black book has to say about subjective crime.

The book told him that: *Anybody who has been sent to*

*prison for a crime that did not involve force, fraud or coercion is not a criminal. The book went on to state that once the anticivilization collapses, these prisoners will be set free or if already set free their subjective crimes will be wiped away from all records.*

This understanding draws a smile across Eschewal's face as he steps out of the airport and up to the cells. Eshewal dwells: *'Yeah, the 'crime' I've committed is subjective. I've not hurt anybody and not planned to force anybody to hurt themselves with the drug or to commit objective crime like street robbery to buy the drug.'*

So feeling that his heart is clean, Eschewal swaggers into the surprisingly clean cell.

# Chapter One Hundred and Fifteen

**ESCHEWAL HAS BEEN LOCKED** in the cell for two hours, due to the capture of other individuals smuggling drugs.

He now sits in the interview room staring at the blank wall. The door opens and two non-threatening officers, stinking of cigarettes and coffee, enter. The taller one is carrying Eschewal's suitcase.

The officers sit down. The one closest to Eschewal presses the record button.

"Interview commencing 15:52. Officer Laurez and Officer Drinkwater. Also detainee Mr Rote is present."

Officer Drinkwater looks up at Eschewal. "Are you Mr Eschewal Rote?"

Eschewal nods his head.

Officer Drinkwater demands: "Please say yes, for the tape recorder."

Eschewal leans forward. "Yes."

Officer Drinkwater continues: "Do the contents in this suitcase belong to you?"

Eschewal leans forward again. "Yes."

"Are you aware that it's illegal to smuggle any substance banned by law under the drugs act?"

Eschewal smiles. "No."

Officers Drinkwater and Laurez look puzzled. Eschewal continues: "I wasn't trying to smuggle it, I was going to declare it. I use cannabis as a healing tea not as a narcotic drug."

The officer's smile. Drinkwater says: "What, all 27 kilos of it?"

Eschewal nods his head. "Yeah, that's about a six-month supply."

Officer Laurez interjects: "Nah, come on son. Make it easy on yourself. You look like a good lad, we know someone must've put you up to this. Just give us the name, and you can get off with maybe a suspended sentence."

Eschewal grits his teeth. He has always known that sentencing for cannabis is lenient. If his eyes could talk they would say to the officers: *"Even if I didn't wanna go to prison I would never snitch or bow down to the system and beg for forgiveness. You're wasting your time because I must plead not guilty to your arbitrary cannabis laws to make sure I'll be put away for at least 3-5 years."*

Eschewal shakes his head. "Nah, like I said, the cannabis is mine. I bought it for personal use. That's all I've got to say, no more comment."

Both officers blow out hot air. Eschewal closes his eyes and drifts off into a state of meditation, while Officer Drinkwater recites: "Okay, we have no choice but to charge you with drug importation under the drugs act. This interview is terminated at 16:10."

The officer stops the tape cassette.

Eschewal crosses his fingers as a smile draws across his face.

# Chapter One Hundred and Sixteen

**THE FOLLOWING DAY IS** bright as Eschewal boards the sweat-box. He arrived at the court at 08:55 He is now standing in the dock at 10:15 before a fat jowled, grey haired judge.

The judge tells Eschewal to sit. The prosecutor stands up and addresses the judge.

He clears his throat. "Your honor, the case against the people's state versus Mr Eschewal Rote is hereby charged under the Narcotics and Drugs Act."

The prosecutor shuffles some papers and continues. "Mr Rote was apprehended by customs officers with 27 kilo grams of cannabis in his possession. He claims the drugs were for his personal use and denies trying to import drugs."

The prosecutor sits down, the judge puts on his glasses and looks over at Eschewal. "Please stand, I see you have no legal representation, would you like to defend yourself?"

Eschewal nods his head. "Yes."

Apathetically, the judge winds out: "Okay go ahead, do you plead guilty or not guilty to the charges."

Eschewal raises his chest. "Not guilty. Because, one, I was not smuggling drugs, I was going to declare it. And two, I do not recognise your subjective arbitrary drug laws.

The only law I recognize is universal law, which is: no person, group of persons, or destructive-governments may initiate force, threat of force or fraud against property or any individual."

Eschewal looks over at the prosecutor then back at the judge and continues: "So, taking in regard that my so called 'crime,' has not breached any universal laws, I am not guilty of any crime, but a man-made agenda driven by subjective law, 'crime'."

Eschewal points at the judge. "Furthermore, the only criminal in this court today is you…"

Eschewal is interrupted by the bang of the judge's hammer, but he continues over it.

"Yes, you're the criminal, you and your cohort politicians who legalise, using fraudulent scientific claims, poisonous addictive drugs such as; sugar and caffeine which they sanction and seep into almost every food that's consumed by young innocent children. Yes, the moment you and destructive-governments disappear is the day everything, which is wrong with this world, will also disappear." Eschewal wipes the corners of his mouth.

The judge looks like he's about to choke with contempt. He takes off his glasses and bangs his hammer of coerced authority even harder. "I beg your pardon? You're in a court of law governed by the law of the land and you shall respect that and throw your mercy upon the court."

The judge flicks over a few pages. "I have no choice but to remand you in custody until a court date is set in front of a jury."

The judge looks over at the court screw. "Take him down."

The screw grips Eschewal and leads him towards the cells. Eschewal follows with a grin on his face. He knew that with his anti-system speech, which he learnt from the black book, the judge would lock him up right away. Eschewal just couldn't risk the judge giving him bail. He had to be locked up now, right now, and flung into ostracism away from his self-destruction, and towards happiness.

# Chapter One Hundred and Seventeen

**AFTER BEING BROUGHT BACK** down to the cells, Eschewal is kept behind lock and key for almost three hours. He had to wait until they had enough bodies to fill the sweat-box. That day only two people out of 14 made it to bail. The rest will be locked in the same prison with Eschewal, except for one, who had to be brought to a youth prison. The youth almost lost the use of his legs when the judge put him on remand. It was his first offence. He tried to impress his friends by knocking out a shopkeeper, just for laughs, but now he has found himself up for an attempted murder charge.

As the screw brings the youth towards the sweat-box, a wrinkled-faced screw lets Eschewal out of his cell and brings him towards the reception desk. Eschewal and the youth cross paths.

Eschewal takes notice of the youth and thinks: *'Look at him, no older than fourteen, shoulders hunched, looking distorted and with eyes showing regret, slowly being lead into the wide jaws of the beast, that swallows up the ignorant who fall into the many pitfalls laid by the sys-*

*tem itself.'*

Eschewal reaches the desk. A young-faced screw hands him his possessions. Eschewal signs a few papers then is handcuffed to a female screw.

Just before being led away, Eschewal says: "Excuse me, can I get a pencil and some paper, please?"

The officer raises his eyebrow, because people usually ask for a cigarette, so he queries: "What do you want a pencil and paper for? Do you plan to write a letter to God, asking him to get you out of this situation?"

Eschewal doesn't make a reply. The officer huffs and looks under his desk. He hands over a pencil and some paper. Eschewal doesn't say thank you as he is led away to the sweat-box.

# Chapter One Hundred and Eighteen

**BY THE TIME THE** sweat-box drops off the young boy at the youth prison and travels back 80 miles to where Eschewal and the rest of the prisoners will be held, Eschewal has completed the first part of his novel. Eschewal feels he has found his essence, which he hopes will make him into a creator of values and bring him happiness & riches.

The van jerks to a stop. Eschewal looks up and is met with the tall iron prison gates that are attached to even taller solid brick pillars.

The sweat-box enters the prison walls as heavy rain begins to fall out of a pitch black sky. Eschewal shakes his head, knowing he has reached hell and will be here for a while until he makes it to his heaven.

As Eschewal steps off the sweat-box, the first thing he sees are the small iron windows; behind them are cramped cells. Below the windows are lines of rubbish that the inmates throw out.

The next thing to hit Eschewal as he walks through the large corridors is the stink of the place; the stench is almost unbearable. It gets no better when he reaches his cell. Luckily, for this one night and this one night only, Eschewal is put in a cell by himself, which means he does not have to endure the stink from another cell-mate.

Eschewal sits down on the iron bed holding his stomach. The food has run out so he has to go to sleep hungry.

Eschewal is about to close his eyes, when he hears: BANG! BANG! BANG!

Eschewal's heart begins pounding.

BANG! BANG! BANG!

"Oi, next door," says an angry voice. Eschewal is about to answer. He pauses when he hears from another angry voice: "Yeah what?!"

The other voice replies: "Are you listening?"

"Yeah go on," says the other.

"Oi, send man a line."

"Send man a line of what, man?"

"Send, man a burn, init."

"Man ain't got no burn, man."

"What, how you mean, man ain't got no burn? Send man a skinny one, man."

"Listen man, lock off, man, man ain't got no burn. You listening, get your head down, man. Ride your bang up, you waste-man."

"How you mean ride my bang up, you dick-head, you better mind I don't bang you up in the showers tomorrow. Oi, don't let me have to weigh you in, you know. I'll kick your face ugly, blud."

"What?! Alright, tomorrow in the showers, you

~ 336 ~

dick-head, you waste-man."

Eventually the whole prison falls quiet. Eschewal stretches out into a sleeping position and closes his eyes. But that night and the 912 nights that follow he does not dream.

# EPILOGUE

# NINE HUNRED AND TWEVLE NIGHTS LATER

# Chapter One Hundred and Nineteen

**THE MORNING PRISON BELL** rings out long and loud, waking up every sleeping body on the wing, except Eschewal. He has already been up for one hour.

It seems like just yesterday Eschewal entered into prison life; fell asleep with a hungry belly and worried about switching back on the old him that got him through the mean streets. As it turned out, prison was not so violent after all. It only became violent for those who either were hooked on drugs, liked to gamble or borrowed things and could not pay back the double-bubble. Apart from that, Eschewal realised he could easily survive behind those steel bars, without having almost any bother. Eschewal did just that; he thanked the black book for cutting him loose from his mysticisms. He had wondered when the purpose of giving up gambling, drugs and other destructions would have its direct benefit.

Eschewal sailed smoothly through the two and half years, reading and writing every single day, rain or shine. In the end, Eschewal had studied the black book to a high level of understanding and read almost the whole prison library and completed two novels and a screenplay with pencil and paper. Eschewal had also got his body into top condition and felt great but he began to feel real happiness everyday that he sat down and created a new chapter in his book. It gave him immense stimulation, similar to what he felt when he had Manna in his arms. *'Manna,'* thinks Eschewal, *'the one and only girl who can complete my life. That one girl to share and reflect my happiness. That one girl, if I was given one wish, would still be Manna.'*

Eschewal is unaware he made a similar wish when he was five; this is the first time he and Manna met... It's a hot summer, the local park is full of mothers and children. Eschewal spots Manna and feels emotions he has never felt before, but it's a simple time, way before Eschewal was being abused and became bad. So he runs up to Manna and begins playing kiss chase. When it's time for Manna to go, he holds onto her hand. Manna and Eschewal begin crying. The mothers say: *"Aww ain't that cute,"* then dry their children's tears. Eschewal's mother takes a picture of him and Manna. Their smiles almost stretch across the picture as Eschewal wraps his arm over Manna's shoulder. After, Eschewal's mother writes on the back of the picture: *Manna, Eschewal's 1st puppy love!* She plans on showing Eschewal the picture once he has grown up, but unfortunately a house fire causes her to lose all her possessions, memories and a six-month-old daughter.

# Chapter One Hundred and Twenty

**ESCHEWAL RAISES HIS HEAD** as the noise from the opening of the cell doors come to him.

CLICK-CLACK! "Morning," CLICK-CLACK! "Morning," repeats the officer as he opens up each cell door individually.

CLICK, CLACK! The officer reaches Eschewal's cell, "MORNING, ROTE," he bellows.

Eschewal turns his head. "Alright, guv?"

"Have you packed your kit?"

Eschewal nods his head to the officer.

"Okay, reception is running late so they won't be ready until after breakfast."

Eschewal nods his head. "Alright, guv," he says, while donning a pissed off look because he was told that he would be leaving an hour before breakfast.

CLICK-CLACK! "Morning," continues the officer down the landing.

Eschewal's door is pushed open once again. A small man with long shabby hair pokes his head through. His name is Jest. He enters with a smile and humor in his voice. "Shit, they haven't changed their minds have they, letting you out?"

Eschewal stretches. "Nah, bruv. Reception is running late, init. They won't be ready till after breakfast."

Jest moves further in the cell. "Have you had your last breakfast? You better have, just to make sure you don't come back to eat it."

Eschewal dwells for a moment on Jest's 'last breakfast' superstition. He shakes his head. Eschewal exposed the destructive matrix of corrupt forces to Jest but the black book is right; some people do not want to be disconnected. Eschewal learned Jest is one of them and realises the underlying reason why he doesn't want to be disconnected. This is because Jest has invested heavily in the destructive matrix of corrupt forces and to Jest there is no turning back. This makes Eschewal so sad to see a potential genius trapped in a mode of thinking that revolves around destruction and death.

Eschewal stands up. "Nah, these bastards ain't never seeing me again," says Eschewal finally.

Jest nods his head and with conviction. He says: "Right you are, bruv, don't make them ever see you again."

Eschewal gets up from the bed. "Oi, eya, bruv. I saved this for you." Eschewal gives Jest his radio, shower slippers and the black book.

"Thanks, mate. I'm gonna read this." says Jest as he clutches the black book.

Eschewal nods his head. "Just remember what I've told you, Jest. You're the creator of your own destiny."

Jest's eyes light up, similar to that of a child's but as usual the exhilaration quickly disappears as Jest remembers his hopeless past and the grey walls, which now surround him.

Eschewal's heart drops as he sees the light go back out in Jest. He then smiles at knowing someday the words from the black book will send a spark out of Jest's sub-consciousness and give him the ability to disconnect from the destructive matrix of corrupt forces.

Eschewal's surname is hollered. Jest looks at him. "I guess they're ready for you."

"Yeah." Eschewal picks up his belongings. "Alright, bruv take care, yeah and remember read the book." He embraces Jest then steps out of his cell and makes his way to reception.

# Chapter One Hundred and Twenty-One

**THE SUN IS SHINING,** the atmosphere is cool. Eschewal has been waiting at the reception desk for five minutes. He is just about to make up noise when the reception officer appears.

"Mr Rote?"

Eschewal nods his head. The officer plonks a large plastic bag onto the desk, which contains a medium-sized bag, some clothes and shoes.

"Sign these papers." The officer pushes over three different forms that are supposed to hold Eschewal to three different conditions which if breached, would send him back to prison.

Eschewal quickly reads through each form then happily signs them, for he knows these conditions will not be able to put him in jeopardy. Prison will never see him again, unless he wants it to.

Eschewal pushes back the signed forms. The officer pushes him his belongings.

"Nah, keep the clothes and shoes. I want to donate them, just give me my bag."

The officer removes the bag and gives it to Eschewal who puts it over his shoulder and waits for the money he has earned while working in the prison. The total has amounted to two grand. The officer counts out the money then stuffs it into an envelope. Eschewal does not say thank you, he puts the money in his bag and heads for the entrance.

As Eschewal reaches the staircase, the officer says in a patronising tone: "Make sure when you come back, you bring a friend."

Eschewal doesn't reply or turn his head. He steadily holds his rage and walks up the flight of concrete stairs towards his freedom. As he reaches the top, sadness consumes him as he remembers his childhood. That bright-eyed little boy who told his grandma he wanted to become a doctor. Eschewal always knew he had a good heart and always felt sick when he had done wrong. Every time he went against his nature, it always cut away a piece of his soul. However, Eschewal feels now he understands everything for what it was. He thinks: *All my beliefs, past actions, before I read the black book; having sex with my auntie, robbing, smoking, doing hard drugs, believing that the black book would bring me effortless riches. And after reading the black book; disconnecting from the destructive matrix of corrupt forces, searching for Manna, falling in love with Manna and becoming the creator of values, were all connected to one common denominator — the need for stimulation and the hope of receiving happiness.*

The old man's warm eyes flicker through Eschewal's mind. He smiles as he remembers thinking the black book was magic. *"Nah,"* he says to him-self, *"The black book was showing me that I'm magic with tremendous potential to create my destiny and achieve what has eluded me for over two decades: real happiness."*

A smirk of enlightenment dons Eschewal's face as his subconscious recalls what the old man was saying while he was staring at the book's title.

The old man had said: *"This book is the system's greatest threat, because it will make you become a thinker. They don't want this because if you begin to think you will begin to see through their evil illusions and their matrix of lies.*

*Not only that, when you become a thinker you can solve your own problems without using their bogus psychologists who do you more harm than good.*

*But the ultimate benefit of thinking gives you the ability to create new values, which will then deliver your reward in the form of happiness, love and riches. But you must take action, read as many books as you can, because readers become thinkers, thinkers become creators of values."*

Eschewal pushes open the tall oak doors and the sunlight hits him. He dwells: *'The greatest drug of all — creating values — holds the key to wipe away poverty, crime, death; and sweep in love, happiness & riches.'*

The door swings shut, as Eschewal is sucked into the light.

Von Mozar hopes you have enjoyed SEXFIEND and will support him further in his goal to get more young people into reading.

Please spread the word about this genre of literature (Hip-Hop/Street literature).

Look out for Von Mozar's third title, Little Jamaica.


Thank you.

Waterbuck publishing invites you to leave your comments on the website: waterbuck.co.uk

# GLOSSARY

| | |
|---|---|
| BAD-MIND | Expressing bad thoughts |
| BALLER | A person with lots of money |
| BANG, BANGED | Sex, Sexed |
| BANGING | Nice |
| BATTY/ BATTY WASH | Buttocks/Oral-anal sex |
| BATTERY | Taking turns to have sex |
| BEAT UP | Sex |
| BER | Many |
| BLING | Running game/deception |
| BLOW | Leave |
| BLUD | A friend |
| BOOMEE | Scared |
| BOPS BOPPING | Walking |
| BREDDRIN | Brethren (a close friend) |
| BRES | Men |
| BRO | Brother/A friend |
| BRUSH | Sex |
| BRUV | Brother/A friend |
| BUCKS | Bump into |
| BUN | Cheat or to have sex with |
| BUS A NUT | Ejaculate |
| BUTTERS | Ugly |
| BOY-DEM | Police, Government, Etc |
| BOOTS | Condoms |
| BREAK LEGS | Being ruthless in competition |
| BS | Bull Shit |

| | |
|---|---|
| CAT | Drug addict |
| CHEESY | Smelly |
| CHIRPSING, CHIRPS | To chat up the opposite sex |
| CHOONG | Nice |
| CHOP | Sex |
| COCK BOTTOM | Extremely curvy backside |
| COCK BLOCKING | Getting in the way of sex |
| CLOCKS | Sees |
| COLD | Can be used as good or bad |
| COP | Buy |
| CRISS | Good or good looking |
| DAT | That |
| DEM | Them |
| DOH | Though |
| DOUBLE BUBBLE | Credit Interest |
| ENDS | Area, location |
| FAM | Short for family (friend) |
| FIRE BUN | To express defiance |
| FUCKRIE | Out of order/wrong |
| FULL HUNDRED | The whole story |
| GALIST | Womaniser |
| GASSED, GASSING | Hype, excited |
| GEE | Gangster |
| GIRL'S MAN | Womanizer |
| GONNA | Going to |
| GO THRU | Sex |
| GREASY | Bad |
| GREENS | Cannabis |
| GWANING | Going |

| | |
|---|---|
| GYAL | Girl |
| HAIRS | Sex |
| HEAD | Oral Sex |
| HEAVY | Good |
| HIT IT | Sex |
| JEZZY | Jezebel |
| JIGGY | Good |
| I SWEAR DOWN | Honestly |
| KETTLE | Wristwatch |
| KILL IT | Sex |
| LAOW | Allow |
| LIFT-BOY | Someone being used as a chauffeur |
| LINK | A date or a meeting |
| LINK UP | Meet |
| LONG TING | For a long time |
| MASH | Sex |
| MOVING/MOVE | Hanging out/Making illegal money |
| NOTES | Money |
| OLD FOOT | A mature woman |
| ONE POP | A one night stand |
| PEES | Money |
| PEEL | Robbery |
| PEN | Prison |
| PUM-PUM | Vagina |
| RAMP | Not messing about |
| REDS | A woman's period |
| RIDE | Car |
| ROLL | Travel |

| | |
|---|---|
| S | Shit |
| SHOTTER | Drug seller |
| SCREW | Prison officer or court bailiff |
| SWEAT-BOX | Prison bus |
| SKINNING OUT | Sex |
| SLAP, SLAPPED | Sex, Sexed |
| SLAM | Sex |
| SORT | A good looking person |
| STAR | A friend |
| STICKY | Dangerous |
| SUCK | Rob |
| TEEFING | Thief |
| TER | An expression |
| TING | Pronoun. Also short for: thing |
| TONK | Well built |
| TRUE STORIES | Acknowledging a true statement |
| WAH GWAN? | What is going on? |
| WASTE-MAN, WATSE-CHICK | Loser, Bum |
| WET | Sex |
| WHAT'S POPPING? | What is going on? |
| WHIP | Car |
| WIFEY | Girlfriend |
| WOK | Sex |
| YA-NA | You know |
| YARD | Ones home |
| YUTE | Youth |

# VON MOZAR

# SPECIAL PREVIEW

# IGNORANCE KILLS...

*This excerpt from Ignorance Kills... brings you into the grimy poverty driven world of Brenda, who falls pregnant to her cousin Shun at the age of twelve. Together they pursue a vicious life of crime until it all comes tumbling down when Shun is shot. Estranged from her mother and without a father since the age of six, Brenda is left to the mercy of the ghetto and must find a way to survive its nightmarish reality.*

# Chapter One

**THE WIND BLOWS ICE-COLD** up and around the short white skirt worn by Fasard, with her wide hips, large breasts and jet-black hair.

She pulls her skirt further down her bruised, goose-pimpled thighs. It quickly springs back to its previous position.

Fasard places her left hand on her hip and rubs her belly with the right. She is feeling pissed. For over two hours she's been standing on the block, waiting for cars to stop. They pass her in a blur, speeding through the night, taking no notice. You couldn't see them, but in the corners of her eyes are frozen tears.

A car begins to slow down. Fasard pulls the fake leopard-print fur coat over her belly, hoping to hide the evidence of another innocent life that will drop into destruction. She moves quickly over to the street lamp where it's brighter and opens the coat to reveal some more flesh while using her handbag to hide the lump.

The car comes to a dead halt and the door clicks

open. Fasard jumps in.

"What's up, babes?" she says casually, with the best sexy smile she can manage.

"It ain't nuttin'," replies the driver as he rubs Fasard's belly.

The rehearsed words from prostitute to squeak seem to freeze in Fasard's throat. She had hoped in the dark of the car the squeak wouldn't realise she was pregnant and maybe she'd get away with just giving oral sex.

Fasard braces herself. She thinks the squeak is going to kick her out of the car, unaware that he had heard a pregnant hooker was giving it up on the block and he had come to get some pregnant-sex.

Still rubbing her stretch-marked, pregnant belly, he says in a whisper, "How much?"

"Erm, erm," Fasard stutters, "Suck and sex, erm twenty, and that includes anal." She pauses and opens her legs as the caressing becomes more vigorous. She wants to tell the squeak to stop, she feels like being sick, but she hasn't turned a squeak all night. She bites on her lip, closes her eyes, then continues while breathing more heavily. "Or ten for just a shine."

The squeak mumbles under his foul-smelling breath while he pulls up Fasard's washed-out T-shirt and sucks on her huge swollen nipples.

"Hol' on, hol' on," begins Fasard with a shocked expression, "you just wanna do it right here?"

"Course, man, course," demands the squeak with his thin lips and small rodent-like eyes. He throws a twenty bill at her, pulls out his penis and drags her head towards it.

Within a few moments, his nuts are busting down her throat. Fasard swallows and pulls back; she thinks her job is over and gets ready to leave. The squeak throws another twenty bill and grabs her face for a second time.

# Chapter Two

**THE RAIN IS NOW** coming down heavy.

Fasard's jaw begins to hurt as she sucks in vain, trying to make him come for the second time. The squeak pulls out. At last, Fasard thinks, it's over.

"Oi, open your legs," the squeak says coldly.

*'Go to hell,'* thinks Fasard, but, holding forty bills she's scared he'll take it away.

He penetrates her bareback, with a penis long enough to hit the baby's head. Fasard grabs the seat tightly, her knuckles turning white. She opens her mouth wide and screams out her contraction pains. At first the squeak is unaware; he carries on ruthlessly riding it until a flush of water wets him.

He curses. "Oi, what the rass?" He pulls out his cheesy manhood.

Fasard's head is banging against the car window. Her eyes are bulging, cheeks puffing in and out. She can no longer talk, as screams and low grunts come out instead. Her legs begin to widen and rise at the same time. A wet mass of black hair is protruding between her thighs.

"Oi, wha gwan? Rah shit, the baby!" The squeak panics. "Oi, get your rass-clart self out the car." The squeak stretches over Fasard and clicks open the door.

"No-no, please, help me please," begs Fasard.

A sinister look crosses the squeak's face. "Are you nuts? Get out my car!" He tries pushing her legs over her face, but Fasard holds on for dear life as her screams travel down the empty wet road.

The squeak begins punching and kicking Fasard, cursing incoherently. Fasard can no longer hold on and drops head first into the pouring rain in the late night of December 13th.

# Chapter Three

**COLD RAIN WETS FASARD'S** face; agony makes it twist into a grotesque form. She crawls off the curb backwards until she reaches the bus shelter. Fasard's screams for help penetrate the stillness of the night.

Help is on its way. Fane – slim, tall and bald-headed comes bopping over to her.

"Oi, what the rass did you do?" he accuses.

Fasard's reply is unclear. She is mumbling as she spits phlegm through her nose and mouth.

"Arh, shut up. Get up, man!"

Fasard doesn't move. She points at her belly while trying to catch her breath.

"Oi, did you hear what I said or you're not listening?" Fane gives her one to the head. "Get up. Are you stupid? What's wrong with you?"

Fane drags Fasard up from the ground. "Come on, you stupid bitch. Come on," he yells pulling her away from the bus shelter.

Fasard finally screams out. "Baby, the baby, I'm having the baby!"

The pair stumble to a halt by a lamppost and Fasard holds on for a rest. She grabs her crutch and slides down towards the ground. Fane snatches her up.

"What?! You wanna have the baby on da floor?"

Fasard again slides towards the ground. "Nah, get off me! Just get off me!"

"Arh, you stupid bitch, get up." Fane strong-arms her away from the lamppost towards a grassed area across the road.

Taking small painful steps and still holding her crutch, Fasard tries wriggling out of Fane's grip. "Get off me!" She shouts. "Just, get off me, yeah."

Fane holds Fasard tighter, ignoring her demands and making her slide on her knees a few times before they reach a cockroach-infested house.

# Chapter Four

**FANE BEATS THE DOOR** down. He still has Fasard in an iron grip.

"Come on!" he says to her, as the door, with its crumpling paintwork, opens.

Fane orders a skaghead from the doorway. "Come out the way!" He bundles Fasard towards the floor, which is covered in mess and dirt.

Sweat and rain are pouring off Fasard, but the sweat makes her peel off her clothes. Fasard lies on the floor naked, except for the mini-skirt rolled up under her tits.

In the shadows, bodies circle the room; some piping, others chasing the dragon.

Fane re-enters the room. "What you doing on the floor? I told you to go over to the settee. Oi, Cee-Cee, get up." A skinny cat piping cocaine jumps from the ripped up settee and runs over to a window, holding his crack pipe tightly to his chest.

Fane flicks on the light switch. Brightness floods the

space. A couple of cats cover their eyes and run out of the room.

Fasard spits, "Get away from me," as Fane goes to pick her up from the floor. A couple of deep pushing groans fill the room. Suddenly, an innocent life cries.

The newborn had suffered, but the spirit of this child is one of a warrior. It was holding on for dear life. Maybe if it knew what it was coming into, it would have given up.

The baby has natural beauty, a full head of hair, sparkling eyes and fresh baby skin. It's unaware that the ugliness that surrounds it will fight to destroy it. Nothing will protect it, not even its parents.

They had long ago passed that duty of care over to God, government, society or even the people who were masturbating as they watched the baby enter the world.

The baby's parents view life as a one-way train, heading towards death, which they feel they have no power to stop. Mixing that with their everyday suffering produces suicidal and destructive thinking, leading to evil acts of wickedness upon themselves and others. They don't care if the baby suffers and dies, because they're suffering and have to die too. All they want is for the baby to live long enough to get them free housing and a few quid. Of course, they will hide these evil thoughts from others and pretend that they're only doing 'God's work' by going forth and multiplying. They even think that somehow this 'God's work' could bargain them into an effortless existence called Heaven. But don't get it twisted. They you're dead you're dead, forever. No more drugs, alcohol or sex. Your very being disappears spiritually and physically into nothingness. Only bones remain, disgusting memories and a freed conscious-soul.

## Ignorance Kills... is out now!